Melanie knew she was being seduced

"Run!" her brain urged, but the warning came too late. There was no escaping the arms that held her and the mouth that descended on hers.

"You're a tantalizing little witch," Jason laughed triumphantly. "Your surrender will be adequate compensation for the loss of my freedom!"

Sanity returned. "Your freedom!" Melanie gasped incredulously, pushing him away. "What about the loss of my freedom?" She was trembling. "I wish I'd never set eyes on you. You're arrogant, self-opinionated, and I hate you!"

Jason's strong fingers dragged her back against him. "You may think you hate me," he accused in a harsh voice. "But I know you're not as insensitive to me as you'd like me to believe."

Suddenly nothing made sense anymore, and Melanie turned and fled.

Bitter Enchantment

by

YVONNE WHITTAL

Harlequin Books

TORONTO・LONDON・NEW YORK・AMSTERDAM
SYDNEY・HAMBURG・PARIS・STOCKHOLM

Original hardcover edition published in 1979
by Mills & Boon Limited

ISBN 0-373-02304-9

Harlequin edition published December 1979

Printed in U.S.A.

CHAPTER ONE

MELANIE RYAN sat curled up on the window seat, the tray of tea untouched and forgotten on the low table beside her as she stared dismally through the rain-spattered window at the water gushing from the gutter to wind its way across the lawn towards the lower part of the garden where the cannas flowered for the last time before the winter. It had rained incessantly for the past two days, and had continued to do so throughout her father's funeral that morning.

Between Sister Wilson and herself, they had supported Granny Bridget at the graveside, sheltering her from the rain with their umbrellas, but the strain of it all had been too much for the frail old lady, and Dr Forbes had had to be called in when they arrived back at Greystone Manor an hour later.

Melanie sighed wearily, pushing her fingers through the long strands of silky, corn-coloured hair that waved naturally about her delicate features and curled softly on to her shoulders. She had slept badly the previous night; in fact, she had slept badly since it had become known two weeks ago that her father's business had collapsed. Her father's death two days ago had been totally unexpected, but understandable considering his attachment to the family business.

These events, following so close to one another, had been a blow to both Melanie and her grandmother, but, to Granny Bridget, the sudden death of the son she had always idolised had been the last straw, and she now lay in her room upstairs in a state of induced sleep to ward off the effects of shock. The future looked bleak,

Melanie decided, but after a lengthy discussion with the lawyer, it was almost a miracle to discover that they still had Greystone Manor. She had her job at the textile manufacturers, and between Granny Bridget and herself they would manage to retain Greystone Manor, the home they both loved so dearly.

Greystone Manor was a rambling old house which stood on several acres of ground against a slight rise on the outskirts of Johannesburg. The grounds sloped down towards the gates, and the indigenous shrubs and trees provided the privacy they had always insisted upon in the past. Melanie loved every centimetre of it with a fierceness and pride that matched her grandmother's, and nothing, *nothing* would ever make her part with it.

A knock at the door brought her out of her reverie and Flora, her white apron starched and spotless, announced a Mr Jason Kerr. Melanie stared up into the sympathetic, dark-skinned face of their faithful servant, and frowned. *Jason Kerr.* The name sounded vaguely familiar, but that was all and, nodding briefly, she indicated that he should be shown in.

Rising to her feet and straightening the pleated skirt of her deep blue woollen dress, she was unaware of how well the colour matched her large, heavily lashed eyes; eyes that mirrored instant recognition when her visitor stepped into the living-room and closed the door firmly behind him. She had glimpsed him briefly at the funeral that morning, and had been left with the puzzling impression that he had looked right through her with such intensity that, for a few seconds, she had felt strangely breathless. Now, face to face with him in the large living-room with its old teak furniture, she had the oddest sensation that the air was being drained systematically from her lungs.

Tall, with broad, powerful shoulders, Jason Kerr

advanced towards her with purposeful strides until he seemed to tower over her in the most imposing and frightening manner. His hair was dark, almost black, and his hawk-like features could very easily have been chiselled out of granite, she decided, but it was the piercing quality of his steel-grey eyes, however, that unnerved her the most. They swept down the length of her slender figure in a dissectory manner, stripping her of her confidence, and making her feel like an ill-at-ease teenager instead of the self-assured twenty-three-year-old woman she was.

'I think there must be some mistake,' he said at last, his voice unusually deep and clipped with impatience. 'I asked to see Mrs Bridget Ryan.'

'My grandmother has been heavily sedated, and she won't be seeing anyone for quite some time, Mr Kerr,' she informed him, pulling herself together with an effort. 'Could I perhaps help you in any way?'

His cold glance swept over her disdainfully, and the hard mouth twisted derisively. 'How much do you know of your father's affairs?'

'Enough, I think, to answer any questions you would like to put to me,' Melanie answered him guardedly, her usually soft and warm voice now cool and abrupt as she felt the unaccustomed anger rising within her at Jason Kerr's attitude. Taking a firm grip on herself, she gestured towards the chair behind him. 'Won't you sit down?'

To her relief he obliged, but he refused her offer of something to drink with an impatient wave of a strong, well-shaped hand, and giving her a glimpse of a gold wristwatch beneath the cuff of his immaculate dark grey suit. Here was a man who knew what he wanted, and would leave no stone unturned until he had succeeded in getting the object of his desire, she realised suddenly, and the thought sent an inexplicable tremor along her nerves.

'Did you know that your late father had gambled heavily on the stock market before his death?' his deep voice interrupted her speculating thoughts sharply.

'Yes,' she nodded briefly, clasping her hands in her lap in an effort to steady them. 'He'd been gambling and losing heavily for the past year, I believe, but I fail to see what concern that is of yours, Mr Kerr.'

'I knew your father reasonably well, Miss Ryan. We met occasionally at business luncheons, and so forth,' he replied, ignoring her remark for the present. 'I knew of your father's losses on the stock market, and I knew, too, that he intended ceasing his activities in that field in order to set his business on its feet once more. That's why, when he approached me in a private capacity and asked for a personal loan, I gave it to him.'

For no reason she could explain, Melanie felt herself go cold. 'You—— You mean my father borrowed money from you ... personally?'

'If the loan had come from my company, my liaison officer would have settled the matter with your father's lawyers, and I would not have suffered the inconvenience of being here today.'

His statement was made harshly and baldly, and Melanie was left in no doubt that he had far better things to do than to find himself seated in their cold and dreary living-room on a rainy March afternoon. He was there unwillingly, and the reason for this she still had to discover as she voiced the question that hovered menacingly in the air between them.

'How much did my father borrow from you?'

'Thirty-five thousand rand,' his reply came without hesitation, and Melanie felt as though she had received a blow against the most vulnerable spot on her diaphragm.

'Dear heaven ...' she groaned, a frantic mental calculation making it agonisingly clear that, after selling the few pieces of jewellery she had inherited from her mother, she would most likely have to spend the rest of her life paying off her father's debt.

'You don't possess that kind of money, do you, Miss Ryan,' his harsh voice cut across her thoughts, stating a fact rather than a query, and she clutched nervously at the arms of her chair as she met his cold, calculating glance.

'My father's personal insurances will barely cover his business debts, and I'm afraid that what you see here,' she gestured expressively as if embracing the entire house, '... is the sum total of what my grandmother and I own.'

The ticking of the ornately carved clock above the mantelshelf seemed to grow louder during the ensuing silence. Jason Kerr sat perfectly still in his chair, watching her through narrowed eyes, but Melanie sensed the pent-up energy in that large, muscular body, as if every muscle was geared for action; waiting, like a predatory animal, for its prey to make the first move. A shudder shook through her slight frame, making her clutch wildly at the arms of her chair once more and, as if accepting this as a signal, Jason Kerr moved as well, removing a large envelope from the inner pocket of his superbly tailored jacket and extending it towards her.

'Perhaps you should take a look at this.'

Melanie supposed afterwards that she should have had some premonition as to the contents of that important-looking envelope, but she had suspected nothing, and the information had shattered her world into fragments about her. Her father had offered Greystone Manor as security for the sizeable loan he was accepting from Jason Kerr. All the necessary papers were there, duly signed and witnessed to the effect that, if something should happen to Hubert Ryan before the loan was repaid, Greystone Manor was to be sold and, from the proceeds of this sale, the said amount should be paid over to Jason Kerr, and the remainder to Bridget Ryan and Melanie, which would enable them to purchase a smaller, more comfortable home.

White to the lips, with the delicate network of veins clearly visible at her temples, she extended the envelope with its unacceptable contents towards the man seated opposite her, but her hand shook so much that it almost fell from her fingers before he took possession of it and returned it to his jacket pocket.

'Mr Kerr . . .' she began with difficulty, swallowing at the constriction in her throat. 'Is that what you intend to do? Sell our home in order to collect the money owing to you?'

'Can you suggest another alternative?' he demanded, raising a censorious eyebrow.

His self-assured manner triggered off her anger. How *dared* he sit there looking so cool and disinterested while Granny Bridget and herself were faced with losing the home they loved and cherished?

'My father had no right to offer Greystone Manor as security, and you had no right to accept it!' she cried angrily, jumping to her feet and pacing the floor with her arms wrapped about herself as if they offered her some protection.

'In business deals, Miss Ryan, there's no limit to what one can offer or accept as security,' Jason Kerr told her impatiently, rising to his feet and placing her at an immediate disadvantage once more, for she had to crane her neck uncomfortably to meet his cold, penetrating glance. 'Any lawyer will tell you that I have every right to take possession of this house in order to collect the amount owing to me.'

'But it's our *home*!'

'And it's *my* money which was used in order to settle some of your father's accounts,' he bit out the words, and Melanie flinched visibly. 'Perhaps it would be better if I called some other time and spoke to your grandmother,' he continued abruptly, and strode towards the door.

'No!' She was beside him in an instant, her eyes large and frightened in her pale face. 'The knowledge that the home she loves is in jeopardy would kill my grandmother. Please, Mr Kerr ... give me time to think this out. I might ... just manage to get the money elsewhere.'

His eyes narrowed perceptibly, and Melanie thought for a moment he would refuse, but he nodded briefly, accepting her request. 'I'll give you a week, then I'll call on you again.'

'I ... could you suggest a meeting place elsewhere?' she suggested haltingly, her desire to keep this matter from her grandmother stronger than her embarrassment at having to arrange a rendezvous elsewhere with this uncompromising stranger. 'My grandmother ... I don't ...'

'My office,' he intervened abruptly with a faint glimmer of understanding as he thrust his card into her hands. 'Next Friday at two-thirty.'

Long after Jason Kerr had gone, Melanie could still feel his forceful presence in the living-room, and the card which he had thrust so unceremoniously into her hand told her why his name had sounded so familiar to her at first. It she had not been so tired and distraught with grief, she might have recalled that there had been enough in the newspapers over the past three years about Jason Kerr to excite the dullest imagination. Wealthy managing director of the Cyma Engineering company, and in his late thirties, he was considered by some as a connoisseur of women, and by others as a man with a razor-sharp brain who never failed to seize an opportunity when he saw one. Influential, and often ruthless, he was a man who commanded respect and, occasionally, fear.

Fear! That was what Melanie experienced at that moment. Fear of what it would do to Granny Bridget's fast crumbling world to discover that Jason Kerr had it in his power to take from her the only remaining thing she loved ... Greystone Manor!

Sister Wilson, slender for her forty years, rose from the chair beside the old-fashioned bed with its heavy drapes as Melanie quietly entered the darkened room.

'How is she?' Melanie asked softly.

'Sleeping peacefully, as you can see,' Sister Wilson replied calmly. 'It's the best thing for her at the moment.'

Melanie nodded silently and approached the bed to take possession of the thin, fragile hand that lay supine above the covers. Her fingers absently traced the dark blue veins running from knuckles to wrist before she pressed her grandmother's hand against her cold cheek, her anxious eyes searching the thin, wrinkled face against the pillow and finding it relaxed in the blessed relief of oblivion.

If only she could find a similar relief, Melanie thought with a twinge of envy. Relief from her own grief, and this new threat that hung over their heads. Since the news of her father's death she had been unable to shed a tear, and they had remained locked in her breast, weighing her down with a leadenness that left her listless and tired.

'You could do with some rest as well,' Sister Wilson remarked, almost as if she sensed the exhaustion coursing through Melanie's limbs.

'I'll be all right,' Melanie assured her, replacing the

hand she held on to the covers and lingering for a moment longer beside her grandmother's bed. 'There's so much still to do,' she added, thinking of all the papers in her father's study which still had to be waded through.

'And plenty of time to do it in,' Sister Wilson insisted gently, but Melanie shook her head firmly.

'I must get my father's affairs sorted out as soon as possible.'

'That's an arduous task which has been placed upon your small shoulders, if you'll forgive me saying so,' the older woman replied frowningly.

'I'll manage,' Melanie answered her with a tired smile as she left the room as silently as she had entered it. 'I'll manage,' she repeated to herself a little more grimly as she went down the stairs and entered her father's study. 'I'll manage, if it's the last thing I do!'

There was no time to lose, she decided as she emptied the first drawer on to the desk. She had a week; a week in which to find thirty-five thousand rand and, somewhere among all these papers, she hoped to find something with which she could accomplish the seemingly impossible.

Melanie worked steadily throughout the afternoon until dinner time that evening, sifting methodically through endless bits of paper and files of correspondence. So far she had come up with nothing of importance, but there were still several drawers and cupboards to go through before she would admit defeat.

She sat down to a solitary meal in the dining-room, but her plate was eventually returned, practically untouched, to the kitchen, with Flora muttering something in Zulu to the effect that Melanie would soon be nothing more than a shadow if someone did not do something about it.

Helping herself to another cup of coffee, Melanie returned to the study and sat staring broodingly at the sheaf of papers before her while she sipped her coffee. What was she going to do if she found nothing among her father's papers with which she could prevent Jason Kerr from selling Greystone Manor? Would he carry out the agreement signed by her father without the slightest compunction?

'Yes, he would!' she muttered aloud, his chiselled, unrelenting features flashing before her tired eyes as she returned her cup to the saucer with a clatter and passed a weary hand across her brow. Men like Jason Kerr did not reach the heights of their profession by re-treating sympathetically in the face of someone else's loss, and it was more than likely that not even the frailty of an old woman would deter him from the steps he intended taking.

Burying her face in her hands, she leaned her elbows on the desk, and it was in this utterly dejected position that Adrian Louw found her some minutes later.

'Have I chosen the wrong moment to pay you a visit?' he asked, putting his head around the study door and taking in the papers strewn across the large mahogany desk.

'No, Adrian,' she assured him with a brief smile, re-maining seated as he stepped into the room and closed the door quietly behind him. 'I could do with a bit of company at the moment,' she added.

'I would have come sooner, but I thought you might want to be left alone for a while,' he explained, seating himself on the corner of the desk where she had cleared a space for him.

'That was very sweet and thoughtful of you, Adrian, and I do appreciate it.'

'You look tired,' he remarked after a while, but the next instant he looked rueful. 'That's not very compli-mentary, I know, but I happen to be concerned about you,' he explained away his statement.

Amusement curved Melanie's lips, but did not quite succeed in reaching her eyes. 'There's no need for you to be concerned.'

His fingers tilted her chin upwards, forcing her to meet his hazel eyes. 'When are you going to get it into this pretty little head of yours that I love you?'

'Please, Adrian, I don't——'

'I know, I know,' he interrupted, releasing her with a pained expression on his boyish face. 'This isn't the right time for such a confession, and besides, you love me like a brother,' he took the words right out of her mouth. 'Why is it that every girl I meet thinks of me only in terms of a brother?' he asked of no one in particular.

Melanie stared at him for a moment, taking in his leanness and the coppery tint in his hair. It was not the first time that he had mentioned his love for her, but, try as she would, she was unable to conjure up more than a deep fondness for Adrian. He was fun to be with, but she constantly shied away from the thought of a deeper relationship with him. She should perhaps have ended their friendship when she realised that he was becoming serious, but somehow she never had the heart to do so, and Adrian had continued proposing to her at regular intervals during the past six months.

'One day there'll be a girl who'll think of you only as a husband, and that would be the right girl for you,' she said gently.

'I don't agree with you, but now is not the time to argue about it,' he shrugged, glancing about him and changing the subject. 'What have you been doing?'

'Sorting through my father's personal papers,' she told him with a sigh, her expression becoming guarded as she thought of something. 'Adrian, you're in finance, and perhaps you could clear up a few things for me.'

'You know I'd be only too willing to help you in any way I possibly can,' he replied instantly, lighting a cigarette and blowing the smoke through the corner of his mouth. 'What's the problem?'

'What happens if one wants to make a loan?' she asked without hesitation as she considered the possibility of making a loan elsewhere which would enable her to keep Greystone Manor while at the same time repaying her father's debt to Jason Kerr.

'Are you asking this from a purely theoretical point of view, or ...?'

'Theoretical, of course,' she assured him hastily.

'Well, then it depends on the size of the loan. If it's a small loan there are various organisations one could approach, but if it's a large loan ...'

'Let's say, for argument's sake, that it's a loan of ... thirty thousand rand,' she interrupted cautiously. 'What happens then?'

'Then you'll have to have someone, or something, to stand security for you.'

'When you say "something", do you mean this house, for instance?' Melanie asked, the hopelessness of the situation becoming only too clear to her.

'This house, yes, or any other possession which might cover the amount of the loan,' Adrian drove his point home.

'And if one possesses nothing of value?' she persisted, averting her glance to avoid the question in Adrian's eyes.

'Then one can forget about the loan.'

'I see ...'

While fidgeting with the pile of papers in front of her, Melanie faced the glaring truth. There was nothing she could do to prevent Jason Kerr from selling Greystone Manor. Granted, the property was worth much more than the amount owing to Jason Kerr, and the remainder of the proceeds would at least enable them to set up a home elsewhere, but nothing would ever be able to take the place of the home she had loved since childhood.

'Melanie, you're not in some kind of financial predicament, are you? I mean——' Adrian hesitated, biting his lip as she raised her cool glance to his, then he crushed his cigarette into the ashtray with an angry gesture and rose to his feet to pace the floor with his hands thrust deep into his pockets. 'Damn it, Melanie, I know your father has left things in a bit of a mess, but if it's money you need——'

'Do *you* have thirty thousand rand?' she cut across his words with a hint of mockery in her voice.

'No ...' he shook his head, staring hard at her for a moment. 'But I could get it for you.'

'With Greystone Manor as security?' she demanded, suppressing the desire to laugh a little hysterically.

'Naturally,' Adrian replied firmly, his hazel eyes questioning her. 'You haven't answered me yet. Do you need that kind of money urgently?'

'No,' she lied, unable to confide in him for some reason she could not explain even to herself.

'Sure?' Adrian persisted, eyeing her a little doubtfully.

'Of course I'm sure,' she insisted, directing his thoughts in a different direction by indicating the piles of papers on the desk. 'Give me a hand with these, will you?'

For almost an hour they worked in comparative silence, sorting the papers into sizes and tying them together in neat bundles. With some sort of order restored to the study, Melanie went through to the kitchen to make them a cup of coffee.

'You'll let me know if there's any way in which I can help you?' Adrian persisted, returning briefly to the subject they had discussed as Melanie walked with him through the hall to the front door some time later.

'It's kind of you to say so, Adrian, but——'

'No buts,' he instructed firmly, gripping her shoulders and turning her to face him. 'And that's an order.'

She nodded reluctantly, murmuring her thanks moments before he kissed her lightly on the lips, and then he was gone, sprinting through the rain to where he had parked his old Chev in the driveway. As the lights swept through the gate she closed the door and locked it, depression folding about her like a cloak now that she was alone once more. There was nothing she could do to save Greystone Manor, a little voice kept telling her, but she refused to give up hope until she had gone through every scrap of paper in her father's study.

As she had done every other night during the past few weeks, Melanie slept badly, and dawn found her seated in a chair beside the window, with deep shadows beneath her eyes as she stared out across the silent garden. The rain had ceased during the night, and the wind had died down, but the evidence of the torrential rain they had had over the past two days was clearly seen in the pools of water that refused to drain away into the saturated soil. This was most probably the last time the Reef would have rain before winter set in, and the cold, frosty nights would change the lawn from a succulent green to a drab brown.

Glancing at the clock beside her bed, Melanie noticed with relief that it was after six. The night had passed slowly and relentlessly, and Greystone Manor would at last come alive to greet a new day, but there was no joy in the thought for Melanie as she tightened the belt of her dressing-gown and left her room, her slippers making no sound on the carpeted floor as she walked down the passage to her grandmother's room.

'How is she this morning?' Melanie asked, finding Sister Wilson drawing the curtains aside as she entered the room.

'I'm very much better, thank you, child,' her grandmother replied from the shadows of the bed before Sister Wilson had time to do so.

'Granny Bridget, you had me worried!' Melanie exclaimed, hurrying towards the bed and snapping on the bedside light in order to take a closer look at her grandmother, but the light brought her own features into sharp focus, accentuating the dark smudges beneath her eyes, and the hollows beneath cheekbones which were not normally so prominent.

'You should get Dr Forbes to prescribe something for you as well,' Granny Bridget remarked shrewdly, gesturing with a thin hand that she should sit down on the side of the bed. 'You look as though you haven't shut an eye all night.'

The truth of her statement brought a smile to Melanie's lips. There was seldom anything she could hide from this shrewd old woman, and the necessity to do so had never arisen till now.

'I'll be all right now that I know you're going to be fine.'

'Of course I'm going to be fine,' Bridget Ryan insisted, patting Melanie's hand. 'It isn't any use letting things get one down. Life has to go on, and we still have each other and Greystone Manor. Your fate I can't determine, my dear, but over my dead body will they take Greystone Manor from us.'

Granny Bridget's statement was like a sword thrusting throught Melanie's heart, and fear spread its icy fingers along her veins. It might well be over her grandmother's dead body that Jason Kerr sold Greystone Manor, she thought, and the responsibility weighed heavily on her weary shoulders.

'Gran, why did Daddy start gambling on the stock market?' she asked despairingly, trying to understand the reasoning of the father she had loved and respected.

'Who knows, child, what bug bites a man and induces him to gamble away what he's worked hard to preserve all his life. Perhaps it's the need for power which money can bring, or just plain greed. In your father's case, I wouldn't like to hazard a guess. He's not here to defend himself, poor boy,' the old woman's voice broke slightly and Melanie was instantly contrite.

'I'm sorry, Gran,' she whispered, stroking the grey head and marvelling at the silkiness of the hair beneath her fingertips. 'I shouldn't have mentioned the subject.'

'No, no,' Bridget Ryan insisted with a firmness in her voice once more. 'It's better to talk about the things that trouble us. It never pays to bottle it all up inside until we're fit to explode.'

Melanie leaned forward and kissed her spontaneously on her wrinkled cheek. 'You're a darling, Granny Bridget, and I don't know what I would have done without you.'

'I don't know what I would have done without *you*, my child. And you, Sister Wilson,' she added as the sister appeared at the other side of her bed to take her pulse. 'You've both been so good to me.'

'No more talking now,' Sister Wilson brushed aside the compliment. 'You must rest, Mrs Ryan.'

'And I must go and get dressed.' Melanie rose reluctantly. 'See you later, Gran.'

Bathed and dressed in a pair of old slacks and sweater, Melanie made her way downstairs an hour later. A slice of toast and a cup of coffee was all she could manage for breakfast while her grandmother's statement kept revolving through her mind.

'Over my dead body will they take Greystone Manor from us.'

Over my dead body!

Melanie moaned softly, burying her face in her hands. What was she going to do if she found nothing with which to prevent Jason Kerr from carrying out her father's instructions? Would he be lenient if circumstances were explained to him, or would he do what had to be done regardless of the consequences?

To give up Greystone Manor would not be easy, but the fear of what it would do to her grandmother was far greater. She had to do *something*. She had to find a solution to the problem ... but where? ... and how? Somewhere among her father's papers there *had* to be something everyone had overlooked, and she could only pray that, if there was something, she would find it, and find it soon!

CHAPTER TWO

THE taxi drove off at speed and Melanie swallowed hard as she turned to stare up at the building before her. Somewhere inside that mass of concrete and steel Jason Kerr was awaiting her arrival, and she did not relish the idea of confronting him with the news of her fruitless search through her father's personal papers. Out of sheer desperation she had called on her father's lawyer the previous day, but their discussion had merely confirmed what she had already known. Greystone Manor would have to be sold in order to settle her father's debt, unless she could persuade Jason Kerr otherwise.

Mechanised glass doors slid open silently at her approach and, after she had made an enquiry at the desk, the lift bore her up to Jason Kerr's private sanctum on the tenth floor at a nauseating speed. With a heart that drummed loudly against her ribs, Melanie walked across the carpeted floor towards the elderly but elegantly dressed woman seated at the desk behind the glass partition. She gave her name and, moments later, found herself ushered into Jason Kerr's large office. The man himself rose behind his desk at her entrance and, with his back to the window, she was alarmingly aware of his height and breadth as she approached him, her footsteps silenced by the thick pile beneath her feet. He gestured abruptly towards the straight-backed chair, and only then did she realise how shaky her legs were as she lowered herself into it and watched him seat himself once more in the padded swivel chair behind his desk.

'I think it would be preferable if we don't waste time with preliminaries and get to the point,' he said abruptly, barely giving her time to compose herself. 'Have you managed to obtain the money elsewhere?'

Melanie would have given anything in the world to have been able to place a cheque for the required amount into the hands of the austere-looking man seated across the desk from her, but she had to admit defeat. 'No, I'm afraid I haven't been able to find that amount elsewhere.'

'Then you leave me no alternative but to do as your father instructed,' he informed her with cold deliberation, pushing back his chair as if the matter was settled, and Melanie knew that she could no longer delay her request for time.

'Mr Kerr ...' she began haltingly, mentally brushing aside the remnants of her pride. 'I love Greystone Manor and would hate to part with it, but for my grandmother's sake, more than mine, I must beg you not to sell our home. Not yet, anyway.'

'I don't think I follow you, Miss Ryan.'

His voice and his manner offered no encouragement, and she lowered her eyes hastily before the intensity of his gaze.

'My grandmother is old, Mr Kerr, and she's not well. Greystone Manor has been her home since she married my grandfather, and she loves every nook and cranny of it. My father's death, and ... everything prior to that has been a tremendous shock to her.' She swallowed nervously. 'If ... if you sell Greystone Manor now, it ... it would mean her certain death.'

Jason Kerr looked slightly incredulous as he picked up his gold pen and twisted it about in his strong, well-shaped hands. 'Are you suggesting that I postpone the selling of your home?'

'Yes, I am,' she replied, lowering her gaze once more

as she added hastily, 'You're quite at liberty, of course, to add interest on to the amount owing to you.'

For a time only the muted sounds of the traffic could be heard, then he dropped his pen on to the blotter and came round his desk towards her, making her aware of the superb cut of his dark suit as it clung to his broad shoulders and slim hips.

'It seems to me you have given this matter a great deal of thought?'

'I had no alternative but to give it a lot of thought,' she admitted, feeling incredibly small as this harsh-faced man towered over her. 'I know how strongly my grandmother feels about Greystone Manor. She hasn't been well lately, and I'm afraid of what another shock might do to her.'

'So what it boils down to is this,' he began, his eyes glittering strangely. 'You want me to wait for an un-limited period ... until after your grandmother's death, to put it bluntly ... before I sell Greystone Manor?'

Hope fluttered faintly in her breast. 'Would you consider it?'

'I might,' came his abrupt reply as he thrust his hands into his pockets and paced the floor with a restlessness she had somehow expected from someone who exuded such energy. 'I presume your grandmother is unaware of this transaction between your late father and myself?'

'She must never know,' Melanie said simply, glancing down at her clenched hands and realising for the first time how tense she was. 'Mr Kerr, would you do as I ask? For an old woman's sake; an old woman whose life is coming swiftly to an end?'

'If I do,' he said at length, ushering her out of the uncomfortable, straight-backed chair into a padded armchair which seemed to enfold her luxuriously, 'then I shall be entitled to some sort of compensation.'

'Compensation?' she blinked up at him confusedly. 'I ... don't think I understand.'

'Don't you?'

His hard mouth twisted derisively, but it was his eyes that gave her her answer in no uncertain terms as they slid slowly and deliberately down the length of her, leaving her with the sickening sensation that she had been stripped systematically of her neat beige suit down to her lace underwear. She had heard too much about him not to grasp his meaning at last, and she drew a deep breath, like someone coming up for air from the depths of the ocean.

'Mr Kerr, you're not asking me to . . . to . . . ?'

'To become my mistress?' he filled in for her blandly, a hint of mockery in his glance as he observed her heightened colour. 'Would you?'

'No!' she bit out the word. 'Never!'

'I thought not,' Jason Kerr remarked calmly in the wake of her outburst, seating himself on the arm of the chair close to her and extending his cigarette case towards her. Melanie declined with a shake of her head, and he lit one for himself, blowing the smoke through his nostrils. 'No, Miss Ryan,' he continued at last. 'The compensation I'm seeking is marriage. Marry me, and your grandmother remains at Greystone Manor for as long as she lives.'

Melanie's heart lurched sickeningly, and she clutched wildly at the edge of her seat as the room tilted dangerously about her.

'You're not serious,' she managed hoarsely, convinced that he was merely joking in a macabre sort of way, but there was no hint of humour on his harshly chiselled features as she stared anxiously up at him.

'I'm very serious,' he confirmed coldly, but her numbed brain still refused to accept what he was saying.

'But it's preposterous!'

'Is it?' he demanded mater-of-factly as he studied the tip of his cigarette. 'I would call it a very reasonable way of compensating me for being inconvenienced.'

Melanie no longer doubted that he meant every word he was saying, and the coldness of fear washed over her, whipping the colour from her cheeks and accentuating the shadows beneath deep blue eyes which had long since lost their sparkle.

'I presume that, if I agree, you intend it to be a ... a real marriage?' she heard herself ask in a voice that sounded quite unlike her own.

'Naturally.'

'And if I refuse?'

Steel grey eyes narrowed, pinning her ruthlessly to her chair. 'Then Greystone Manor is sold, regardless of the consequences.'

His words found their mark with the accuracy of an arrow finding its target, and Melanie winced inwardly as she felt their impact. 'You drive a hard bargain, Mr Kerr.'

'Bargaining is part of my business,' he reminded her, crushing his cigarette into the steel ashtray beside his chair. 'I know what I want, and I set out to get it, but I still consider my request to be a reasonable one.'

'There's nothing reasonable about it. I hardly know you, and you expect me to ... oh, lord!' She broke off, burying her face in her trembling hands at the thought of what marriage to this granite-faced man would entail. She would be his to do with as he pleased, while Granny Bridget continued her life in peace and serenity at Greystone Manor.

'Don't consider it a life sentence,' he interrupted her thoughts harshly. 'I might have tired of you by the time the house is eventually sold, and then you'll be free to go.' He smiled cynically. 'Divorce is so easy these days.'

'I must have time to think,' she prevaricated.

Jason Kerr flicked back his cuff and glanced at his wristwatch. 'I'll give you ten minutes to think about it.'

'Ten minutes?' she questioned incredulously, a spark

of anger igniting within her and sending the flow of blood more swiftly through her veins.

'How much longer do you need to consider the effect your rejection of my proposal will have on your grandmother?' he demanded in a clipped voice, rising to his feet and walking across to the other side of the room. He pressed a concealed button and, to Melanie's astonishment, a section of the panelled wall slid inwards and to the side to reveal a drinks cabinet. He poured something into two glasses and splashed soda water into one before returning to her side. 'Drink this,' he said, pressing a glass into her hand. 'It may settle your nerves and make you see sense.'

Her hand shook to such an extent that she brought the glass hastily to her lips and swallowed a mouthful, realising too late that it was brandy. She coughed and gasped for breath as the fiery liquid slid down her throat and, to her embarrassment, her eyes filled with tears. Setting down her glass, she glimpsed a hint of humour in his glance, and her anger flared instantly.

'I wish I could tell you to go to the devil and do your worst!' she snapped as she found her handkerchief and dabbed at her eyes.

'I have no doubt that you do wish that,' he countered swiftly, 'but your conscience wouldn't allow it. It would save time if you gave me the answer I want, Melanie.'

For some inexplicable reason his use of her name suggested an intimacy that sent an unwelcome tremor along her nerves. 'I have no choice, have I?'

'None whatsoever.'

'Then you don't need me to tell you what my answer must be.'

He stared hard at her for a moment, making her feel like an insect wriggling on a pin, then he moved his shoulders slightly beneath the expensively tailored jacket, and swallowed down the remainder of his drink.

'I shall contact your employer at the textile manufacturers and arrange for you to be released next Friday,'
he said in a businesslike voice, and Melanie's startled
glance met his.

'How do you know where I work?'

'My dear child, I haven't been idle this past week,' he
mocked her. 'While you were investigating your father's
affairs, I was investigating you.'

'Why?' she demanded indignantly. 'Did you imagine
that I would ignore my father's debts and steal off into
the night, or something equally distasteful?'

'No,' he said firmly. 'You have too much pride and
strength of character to even consider such a cowardly
act.'

His observation surprised her. 'If you knew that, then
why did you have me investigated?'

'You interested me, and that's why I made it my business to find out all there was to know about you.' He
smiled briefly, and the tension increased within her as
she glimpsed that hint of sensuality about his seemingly
flexible mouth. 'I know that you're twenty-three, and
that your mother died shortly after you were born. Your
father never remarried and your grandmother virtually
brought you up single-handed. I also know that you've
been seeing quite a lot of a chap by the name of Adrian
Louw, and that, if it depended on him alone, you would
have married him.' Her gasp of astonishment made
him pause momentarily before he added smoothly.
'There's very little I don't know about you, Melanie
Ryan, and what I don't know I aim to find out after
our marriage.'

His meaning was only too clear and, cheeks flaming,
she averted her glance to avoid the penetrating quality
of his eyes. 'I'm certain a great many women have interested you in the past.'

'I don't deny that.'

'Neither am I unaware of your reputation where women are concerned,' she said before she could stop herself, and a flicker of amusement flashed across his face; amusement which was directed at her, and which sent the blood surging back into her cheeks.

'I've never hidden the fact that I don't live the life of a celibate,' he announced in his unperturbed fashion. 'Just as I've never pretended an interest in marriage.'

'What made you decide to break that rule on this occasion?' she asked, despising herself for her curiosity.

'Rules were made to be broken occasionally, as in this instance. I knew you wouldn't give me what I wanted without the legality of a marriage certificate.'

'Must you be so crude?' she gasped, making the mistake of jumping to her feet, for Jason Kerr stood up at the same time, and she suddenly found herself so close to him that their bodies were almost touching in the confined space between their chairs. Her nerves vibrated at his nearness and, as if sensing the panic that rose sharply within her, he smiled with cynical amusement as she moved hastily away.

'I believe in plain speaking, then everyone knows where they stand, but let's get back to the subject under discussion,' he continued as if nothing had happened. 'I shall make all the necessary arrangements for us to be married next Saturday.'

'Next Saturday? But that's too soon!' she cried, fighting against the net that seemed to be closing in on her with such speed. 'That's only a week away, and I don't——'

'From now on I call the tune, Melanie Ryan,' Jason Kerr interrupted harshly, and just one glance at his formidable countenance made her realise with what ease he could bend her to his will.

'What do you think my grandmother will have to

say when I confront her with the news of our hasty marriage?' she tried once more.

'You'll have to convince her that this is not as sudden as it seems, and leave the rest to me.'

Melanie's throat felt curiously dry, and she swallowed with difficulty. 'Mr Kerr——'

'Jason,' he interrupted her smoothly. 'You'll have to start calling me Jason if you want to sound at all convincing.'

The unreality of the situation she had landed herself into suddenly hit her with the force of a sledgehammer, and she felt herself reeling mentally under the impact. In order to protect Granny Bridget, she had placed herself within Jason Kerr's power, and he intended wielding that power without the slightest sign of mercy, it seemed.

Closing her eyes for a moment against the onslaught of his rapier-sharp eyes, she whispered pleadingly, 'Please tell me this is some sort of nightmare I'm having?'

She had not meant to speak her thoughts aloud, and she somehow expected a barrage of cynicism, but she was certainly unprepared for the crushing strength of his muscular arms and the bruising hardness of his mouth against her own. Alarm pulsed through her veins, but before she could react, she was set free.

'Did that make it a little more realistic for you?'

With her head spinning and her nervous system in complete disorder, she clutched wildly at the back of a chair for support, her fingers digging into the padded leather upholstery. 'That was unnecessary,' she croaked angrily.

'You'll have to get used to my kisses, and the sooner the better,' he instructed callously, picking up her hand-bag and handing it to her before taking her arm and propelling her towards the door. 'And to add to the realism, I'm taking you out to buy an engagement ring.'

Her protests died on her lips as he glanced at her sharply, and she walked beside him in silence as they approached his secretary's desk.

'Mrs Howard, I would like you to meet my fiancée, Melanie Ryan.'

Mrs Howard's eyebrows rose a fraction at Jason's introduction, but she controlled herself admirably and smiled with unaffected warmth at Melanie, murmuring her congratulations before returning her attention to her employer.

'Are you going out, Mr Kerr?'

Jason nodded briefly in the affirmative. 'Cancel my appointments for the rest of the afternoon, and if Miss Cummings telephones, tell her I shall see her this evening.'

'Very well, Mr Kerr.'

Melanie wondered vaguely who 'Miss Cummings' was, but Jason hurried her into the lift, and her stomach shot up into her throat, making speech impossible as they were swept down to the basement. She was not in the least surprised when he unlocked the door of a sleek, silver-grey Jaguar and helped her into it. It was to be expected that a man like Jason Kerr would select a car that offered him power as well as comfort.

During the drive from the industrial area to the city centre, Melanie maintained the silence between them, but, in the confined space of the car, she found herself becoming increasingly aware of him. His strong hands rested lightly and confidently on the steering wheel, giving the impression that, as with everything else, he was in complete control, and she noticed for the first time the fine black hair on the back of his hand and at his wrist, where his gold watch glinted in the sunlight. His profile was stern, she noticed as she glanced at him covertly, the high bridge of his nose and the square chin denoting strength, and his mouth...! She looked away quickly, her heart skipping a beat as she felt again the pressure of his lips against her own. There was a hint of cruelty about his mouth; it was one of the first things she had noticed about him, and she had no doubt that, for Granny Bridget's sake, she would yet experience that cruelty in all its facets.

She fumbled nervously with the seat belt when he eventually parked the car at the entrance to an illustrious jeweller's shop and, frowning with impatience, Jason brushed her hands aside and undid the belt, but his hand inadvertently brushed against her thigh, and she was forced to avert her head swiftly as she felt embarrassment stinging her cheeks.

The next half hour became part of the nightmare as she found herself seated beside Jason with several trays of rings displayed before her. Dazzled by the brilliance of the stones, and feeling more like a prisoner who had been given the honour of selecting his own handcuffs, she shrank physically and mentally from a task which should, under different circumstances, have been accomplished with joyous anticipation.

'Is this really necessary?'

'Very necessary,' Jason replied, his lips tightening ominously. 'A man in my position doesn't become engaged without buying his fiancée an engagement ring.'

'But——'

'Give me your hand.'

It was a command, and she found herself obeying, albeit with some reluctance, but she found difficulty in explaining the sensations that seemed to spiral up her arm as her small hand lay against his warm palm.

While Jason studied her hand and the tray of rings, Melanie took the opportunity to study him, her glance lingering on the dark, heavy eyebrows, and the thick black lashes fringing his eyes. She raised her glance to his short dark hair which was brushed back severely from his broad forehead, and it was with a certain amount of surprise that she noticed the smattering of grey at his temples. He was, after all, in his late thirties, she told herself, but the thought of someone so virilely masculine ageing in the usual manner was almost unacceptable to her.

'This should do,' Jason interrupted her thoughts and, pulling herself together, she glanced down at her hand to find him placing a ring on her finger that was beautiful enough to make the most reluctant heart quicken with pleasure.

A large diamond nestled in the centre of the delicate setting with, on either side of it, a deep blue sapphire which was cut slightly smaller. Melanie held her breath, knowing it was expected of her to say something, but finding herself unable to do so.

'The sapphires match your eyes,' Jason remarked, surprising her out of her stunned silence with this knowledge.

'It's beautiful,' she whispered inadequately, aware of his searching glance, but refusing to meet his eyes for fear of the mockery she would see there.

The seconds seemed to tick by endlessly before she felt him move beside her and heard his clipped command to the assistant.

'We'll take it ... as well as the wedding ring.'

The wedding ring! Oh, God! ... would some miracle not save her from this marriage which circumstance was forcing her into? If only her father had not gambled away his possessions so foolishly. If only he had sought a loan elsewhere. If only ... if only...! Futile words that brought only pain and left the past unaltered. The future was what mattered now, and how she would be able to cope with the burden which she had placed so firmly on her own shoulders.

Melanie was in a daze when they finally left the shop.

She was only vaguely aware of climbing into the silver-grey Jaguar, and of Jason's hands fastening the safety belt securely about her. The ring on her finger sparkled and glittered in the afternoon sunlight, awakening her to the stark reality of the situation, and mocking her frantic but feeble thoughts of escape. It was only when the car's tyres crunched up the long driveway of Grey-stone Manor that she made an effort to shake off the fit of depression she had allowed herself to sink into.

'Perhaps it would be better if I saw your grandmother now and got it over with,' Jason suggested as he helped her from the car.

Alarm swept over her as she raised her frightened eyes and met the intense scrutiny of his grey glance. 'I thought I would speak to her alone first, before ...'

'I think not,' he said abruptly, cupping her elbow in his hand and sending that current of awareness surging through her again. 'Come on.'

With her hand on the polished brass knob of the heavy oak door, Melanie hesitated. 'Mr Kerr ... Jason ...'

'I shall behave like an adoring fiancé, have no fear,' he interrupted her, guessing with embarrassing accuracy the reason for her hesitation, and taking diabolical pleasure in increasing her humiliation by adding, 'Just make sure that you respond in a similar fashion.'

With her cheeks flaming and her back rigid with anger, she turned the handle and led the way inside, only just succeeding in composing herself as they entered the living-room to find her grandmother seated in an armchair, with a rug thrown over her knees and the uniformed Sister in attendance.

'Sister Wilson, may we see my grandmother alone for a few minutes?' Melanie asked with a calmness she was far from experiencing as she became aware of Jason's arm about her and the possessive warmth of his hand at her side where she could feel her heart pounding wildly. Surely he must feel it too? she thought nervously.

Sister Wilson glanced from Melanie's flushed face to Jason and back, her smile deepening as she appeared to grasp the situation. 'Of course, my dear. Just ring the bell if you should need me.'

'Granny Bridget ...' Melanie began, escaping from the disturbing circle of Jason's arm as the door closed behind Sister Wilson, and moving towards the old woman's chair. 'I would like you to meet Jason Kerr.'

'Jason Kerr?' Bridget Ryan repeated slowly, her eyes, dulled with age yet nevertheless alert, raised towards the man before her. 'I've heard that name before. You have something to do with Cyma Engineering, don't you?'

'Absolutely correct, Mrs Ryan,' Jason replied as he came forward to take the hand she extended towards him, and Melanie stared in amazement at the transformation in the man standing beside her. With his austere features relaxed into a genuine smile he was actually devilishly attractive, and Melanie's pulse quickened in the most absurd manner.

Jason pulled an armchair closer for Melanie, and she glanced up at him thankfully, but only barely concealed her consternation when he lowered himself on to the arm of her chair. With his thigh brushing against her arm and his hand resting casually on her shoulder, her throat went dry, and she found it extraordinarily difficult to concentrate on what her grandmother was saying.

'What brings you here to Greystone Manor with my granddaughter, Mr Kerr?'

'Gran, Jason and I ...' Melanie plunged into speech, but she found herself unable to continue when her grandmother's glance, widening with dawning comprehension, was directed at her.

'What Melanie is trying to say, Mrs Ryan,' Jason came to her rescue, 'is that we've become engaged, and that we would like your blessing.'

'Engaged?' Bridget Ryan's voice echoed in surprise as she glanced from one to the other. 'Melanie, you never gave any indication that you had such plans?'

'It ... was rather sudden, Gran,' Melanie explained lamely.

'Sudden?'

'Melanie means that we knew from the moment we met that we were meant for each other,' Jason came to her rescue once more. 'Isn't that so, Melanie?'

His fingers caressed the side of her neck in a display of affection that momentarily robbed her of speech, but her lack of response fortunately went unnoticed.

'And when, may I ask, do you plan to be married?' her grandmother was asking.

'Next Saturday,' Jason replied firmly.

'Melanie?' her grandmother queried his statement with surprising calmness. 'Is that what you want?'

A frantic denial hovered perilously on her lips, but the firm pressure of Jason's hand on her shoulder acted as a warning.

'Yes, Gran,' she whispered, managing somehow to smile up at the man seated beside her, although she fumed inwardly at the flicker of triumph in his eyes.

An awkward silence prevailed momentarily and Melanie found herself torn relentlessly between two conflicting emotions; the desperate desire for her grandmother not to suspect that all was not as it should be, and the determination to protect this frail old woman from yet another shock.

'All that remains, then, is for me to congratulate you,' Granny Bridget smiled eventually, extending her thin hands towards them, and Melanie hovered dangerously between laughter and tears.

Sister Wilson was called in a few minutes later and, together with Granny Bridget, they enthused over Melanie's engagement ring. Tea was wheeled into the living-room and Melanie poured, but if anyone noticed her hand shaking when she handed Jason his tea, then it was blamed on the excitement of her coming wedding which became the main topic of conversation. Melanie herself heard very little of what was being said, but when Jason eventually took his leave of her grandmother, she knew that this imperious and austere man had somehow succeeded in charming his way into her grandmother's favour.

Melanie accompanied Jason to the door, but his hand shot out and gripped her wrist before she could open it.

'I presume it will be expected of us to say our farewells here,' he explained softly as she glanced questioningly up into his now cold and impassive face, and she felt her cheeks redden beneath his gaze.

'Does it matter if we don't act according to what is expected of us?' she asked tritely, freeing her hand from his and moving a pace away from him.

Jason's glance was instantly mocking as he said in a lowered voice, 'For the time being we should give the impression that we're behaving in the expected manner ... if you still want your grandmother convinced,' he added with a derisive twist to his lips that sent a shiver of fear through her. 'After our marriage there'll no longer be any need for pretence.'

What exactly he had meant by that remark Melanie could only guess at, but there had been an ominous ring to his words that did nothing to relax the tension that had her in its ruthless grip.

'I'll telephone you on Monday,' he said abruptly and, setting her aside as if she were a worthless parcel of goods which happened to be in his way, he opened the door and closed it softly and decisively behind him.

Melanie stood staring at the door and, following the sound of his footsteps, she could almost see him striding lithely across the marble patio and down the steps towards his car. Moments later the engine sprang to life, then the Jaguar was being driven at speed down the driveway.

Sighing heavily, she was aware that her wrist was still tingling where Jason's fingers had firmly gripped it, but glancing down to see if the imprint of his fingers were still visible, she found her attention captured by the ring he had placed on her finger only that afternoon. If someone had told her at the breakfast table that she would have agreed to marry Jason Kerr before that day had ended, she would have laughed herself silly, but there was no humour in the reality of what had occurred, only a frightening hysteria surging to the surface which she was forced to suppress with a near physical effort as she heard her grandmother calling to her from the living-room.

With her emotions firmly under control, she returned to Granny Bridget's side and smiled down into the wrinkled face with genuine warmth. 'I'm sorry I lingered so long in the hall, Gran.'

'When one is in love, every parting, for however short a period, is an agony,' her grandmother replied with calm understanding that sent the colour rushing back into Melanie's pale cheeks.

So Jason's ruse had worked, she thought with growing embarrassment. By his preventing her from opening the front door immediately, her grandmother and Sister Wilson had been given the impression that she and Jason had spent those few moments in the hall taking passionate leave of each other. Nothing could have been further from the truth, but how were they to know and, taking her silence as the affirmative, the two older women glanced knowingly at each other and smiled whimsically, almost as if they had recalled something from the days of their own youth.

'I approve of your choice, Melanie,' her grandmother continued, completely unaware of her granddaughter's discomfiture. 'Jason Kerr is a man who has no doubt sowed wild oats in his time, but he'll be a husband you can depend on at all times.'

'He's handsome too,' Sister Wilson added with a twinkle in her eyes. 'If I were twenty years younger, Melanie, you might have found me a competitor for his favours.'

Overcome with a feeling of guilt at having fooled them so thoroughly, Melanie forced a smile to her unwilling lips and turned towards the door. 'I must go upstairs and wash my hair.'

'Is Jason taking you out this evening?' Bridget Ryan wanted to know.

Melanie halted in the doorway and shook her head. 'He said he'd telephone me on Monday.'

'Will he be away the weekend, then?' her grandmother persisted, and Melanie realised suddenly how strange it must seem to them that her newly acquired fiancé would not be in attendance during the coming two days.

'Yes,' she said, grasping at her grandmother's suggestion. 'He'll be away on business.'

'Oh, well,' Bridget Ryan sighed sympathetically. 'I dare say you'll have to get used to sharing him with his work.'

'I expect I shall get used to it.'

Unable to keep up the pretence a second longer, Melanie turned and almost ran across the hall, taking the steps two at a time in her desperate hurry to be alone with her thoughts to sort out the dreadful situation she had plunged herself into. Breathless from the unaccustomed exertion, she fell across the bed and buried her face in her arms. It was useless searching for an avenue of escape when she had examined every facet of the situation so thoroughly before approaching Jason Kerr that afternoon.

She had prepared herself to argue with him, even plead, but she had never suspected that he would demand such a high price for his leniency. She could perhaps have refused him and taken the chance that her grandmother would survive yet another shock, but the risk was too great to even contemplate. Jason Kerr knew very well that, with the title deeds of Greystone Manor in his possession, he was in an infallible position to bargain for what he wanted—and the object he desired was herself!

It was an abominable situation to find herself in, but, despite everything, the man intrigued her in the most disturbing way. It was no wonder that women found him fascinating, for he had the power to frighten and excite simultaneously, and very few women could resist such a forceful combination. Melanie had to admit to herself that she was not immune to it either, and she would have to be wary of him in future.

CHAPTER THREE

ADRIAN LOUW'S Chev came up the drive the Saturday afternoon following Melanie's engagement to Jason Kerr, and a few moments later he was sprinting up the steps on to the terrace where she sat sunning herself while brooding over the future.

'Have you seen this?' he demanded, dropping a newspaper into her lap and pushing agitated fingers through his coppery hair as he drew up a cane chair and sat down.

'This' was a photograph of Jason Kerr, suave, immaculate, and looking faintly annoyed with the photographer who had caught him coming out of what appeared to be a restaurant, and the caption read:

'Jason Kerr, much publicised head of Cyma Engineering who, in a recent interview, stated that he was a confirmed bachelor and determined to remain so, has obviously met his match in Miss Melanie Ryan, and the couple announced their engagement yesterday. Mr Kerr, however, was not available for an interview, but rumour has it that the wedding is to be in the very near future.'

There was more, but Melanie lowered the paper with a hollow feeling in her chest. Now that their engagement had been made known to the public, there was no possibility of withdrawing if she did not want to make a spectacle of herself and everyone concerned. If the announcement was Jason's idea, then it was a very clever move, and one she should have expected him to make, for he knew that pride would now prevent her from wriggling out of this situation at the last minute.

'Is it true, Melanie?' Adrian demanded, interrupting her disturbing thoughts.

'Yes, it's true.'

His eyes clouded with pain. 'Why didn't you tell me?'

'I was going to, but ...' She hated herself for not having prepared him for this shock, and gestured helplessly with the newspaper still clutched in one hand. 'Adrian, I had no idea there would be an announcement in the newspaper.'

'Everything Jason Kerr does and says is news these days, and you should have known your engagement was bound to be advertised,' he admonished her, and she lowered her glance guiltily.

'I should have known,' she acknowledged unhappily, 'but I'm afraid I never gave it a thought.'

'How long have you know him?'

'A few weeks,' she said evasively, but Adrian was not satisfied.

'How long *exactly*?' he wanted to know, rescuing the newspaper from being mutilated at her hands, and placing it on the table.

'I ... met him some days ago on the day of my father's funeral.'

'And the wedding?' Adrian persisted. 'When is that to be?'

'A week today.'

'For God's sake, Melanie!' he exploded, making her jump at the sharpness of his voice and the violence of his actions as he jumped to his feet and paced about with his hands thrust deep into the pockets of his grey slacks. 'Do you know what you're doing?'

'I think so, yes,' she told him with a calmness that was beginning to surprise her as he stopped beside her chair and held her glance.

'With the kind of reputation that man has, I'm surprised he didn't just carry you off to one of his many hideouts without tying himself down by marrying you.'

She flushed deeply, and winced at the bitterness in his voice. 'Please, Adrian, don't!'

'You know he has a reputation with women, surely.'

'Yes, I know.'

'And you're still going to marry him?' he wanted to know, lowering his incredulous glance to the ring she was twisting nervously about her finger.

'Yes.'

'My God!' he exclaimed, pushing his fingers through his hair and turning away from her, but not before she had glimpsed the look of pain which had flashed across his face.

'I'm sorry, Adrian,' she apologised inadequately, swinging her legs off the recliner and rising to her feet to touch his arm lightly. 'I really am sorry I have to hurt you in this way, but I never once gave you any reason to hope that our relationship would develop into anything beyond friendship.'

'I know,' he admitted, turning towards her now that he had himself under control, 'but don't you think you're being a little unwise rushing into a marriage with someone you hardly know?'

'I know him well enough to realise that I must ... that I *want* to marry him,' she replied, correcting herself hastily.

'Then there's nothing more to be said, is there,' he stated flatly, gripping her hands tightly as he stood facing her. 'Melanie, if you ever need a friend ...'

'You're very kind, Adrian,' she whispered when he left his sentence unfinished, but she knew he would be the last person she would ever approach with the problems she might encounter in the future.

'I *mean* it,' he stressed his offer, leaning forward unexpectedly to kiss her lightly on the cheek. 'If there's anything I could do for you, you know where to find me.'

He was down the steps and striding towards his car

before she had time to reply, and moments later she found herself alone on the terrace once more, but this time with Jason Kerr's photograph staring up at her from the small table with that hint of annoyance in his eyes; annoyance which almost seemed to be directed at her. Picking up the newspaper, she studied the photograph more closely, but the ruthlessness of his chiselled features made her tremble as she went inside.

The ringing of the telephone brought her hastily into the hall and, to her dismay, she heard a reporter from one of the Sunday newspapers glibly requesting an interview with her.

'I'm afraid it's out of the question,' she told him quite firmly, shrinking inwardly at the mere thought of being questioned by someone about something she had no wish to discuss. 'I suggest you approach Mr Kerr for the information you require.'

'Mr Kerr is not available for comment,' the male voice was quick to inform her.

'Then I'm afraid you'll have to wait until he *is* available.'

'Miss Ryan,' the man continued persuasively, 'it wouldn't hurt to give me fifteen minutes of your time.'

'I'm sorry, but the answer is no!'

'You shan't always be able to shun publicity, Miss Ryan,' the voice warned. 'As Jason Kerr's wife you will soon find yourself as much in the news as he.'

Melanie closed her eyes for a moment as the truth of his statement penetrated her mind with a force that made her sink weakly into the chair beside her. It had never occurred to her that, as Jason's wife, she would be an object of interest to the press, and the realisation did not bear thinking about at that moment.

'Miss Ryan?' the voice at the other end queried as the silence lengthened. 'Are you still there?'

'Yes, I'm still here,' she replied in a voice that

was remarkably cool considering the turmoil of her thoughts.

'Have you changed your mind about the interview?'

'No, I haven't.'

'Will you answer a few questions over the telephone, then?'

'No, I will not!' she exclaimed hotly, astounded at the man's persistence. 'I have nothing to say concerning my engagement to Mr Kerr, and I must ask you not to trouble me again. Goodbye!'

Her hand was shaking as she replaced the receiver firmly on its cradle and went in search of her grandmother, but an hour and half a dozen telephone calls later, she was forced to remove the plug from the wall in order to have a little peace. It seemed as though every reporter from all the newspapers in the city was suddenly clamouring for an interview, and the strain of having to refuse them was beginning to shatter her nerves.

'You can't blame them for trying,' Granny Bridget said calmly. 'Jason Kerr is a man of importance, and the reporters will be failing in their duty if they didn't make an effort to approach you.'

'Are you suggesting that I agree to see them, Gran?' Melanie asked incredulously.

'I'm not suggesting anything, my dear child,' the old woman insisted quietly. 'It's up to you to reject or agree to an interview, but don't blame the reporters for trying, and don't let it upset you unduly.'

Melanie bit her lip nervously. 'I should have known something like this would happen, but I stupidly never gave it a thought.'

'It's a pity Jason is away. He would have known how to handle the situation.'

Melanie was on the point of contradicting her grandmother when she remembered the lie she had told in order to explain away Jason's absence. One lie usually led to another, she thought unhappily, and there would most probably be many occasions in the future when she would have to resort to lies in order to conceal the truth in her marriage.

Bridget Ryan leaned forward in her chair and frowned at the shadows she saw lurking in her grand-daughter's blue eyes. 'Have I said something wrong, child?'

'No, Granny Bridget,' Melanie smiled, pushing a strand of fair hair away from her face. 'I was just wondering to what extent my life will be altered once I'm married.'

'Are you having second thoughts about marrying Jason Kerr?' her grandmother asked with concern. 'You did rather allow yourself to be rushed into it, and I don't think anyone will blame you if you find you need time to reconsider.'

Bridget Ryan was very astute for her age, and Melanie knew that if she wanted to sound at all convincing she would have to make an effort to shake off this fit of depression she had become enmeshed in.

'I wasn't having second thoughts, Gran,' she said eventually, a reassuring smile curving her lips as she left her chair to kneel beside her grandmother's in order to kiss the wrinkled cheek. 'I don't need time to reconsider either.'

'You're very certain of your love for him?'

She should have expected this question to be asked at some time or another, but it shook her considerably at that moment, and it took her several seconds to reply.

'Yes, I'm very certain,' she said softly, guilt staining her cheeks as she kept her glance lowered to the ring Jason had placed so unceremoniously on her finger.

Whether it was the forced sincerity in her voice or the blush on her cheeks that did the convincing, Melanie could not be sure, but her grandmother appeared to be satisfied, and it was with a certain amount of relief that she glanced up to see Sister Wilson entering the sun-room. Without either of them noticing it, the sun had been sinking swiftly, and Melanie shivered now as she watched Sister Wilson take her grandmother's arm and help her inside, but the shiver that went through her became a tremor of fear. In a week's time she would be Mrs Jason Kerr, and God only knew how she would survive the ordeal.

Facing Mr Tanner across his desk that Monday morning, Melanie discovered that the announcement in the newspaper, as well as a call from Jason, had transformed her usually disgruntled employer into a charming and understanding man. Making sure that she was comfortably seated, he congratulated her and proceeded to tell her most politely that, although it was against the company's rules and regulations, he would be happy to accept a week's resignation from her under the circumstances. He went on talking for several minutes, but Melanie was no longer listening as a sickening realisation swept through her. Jason Kerr had used his influence to shatter her final hope of postponing their wedding date. He had won again, she realised as helpless anger stirred within her. He was the hunter out to get what he wanted, and *she* was the panic-stricken animal who had inadvertently fallen into his trap.

Melanie shivered uncontrollably and, back at her own desk some minutes later, she had to force herself to concentrate on her work, thankful for the first time that she was alone in an office and spared the necessity of pretending a happiness she was far from experiencing. Her telephone rang incessantly that morning and, although they were mostly business calls, her nerves reacted violently on each occasion before settling down to normality when the voice at the other end was not Jason's. When he did eventually telephone her, her heart seemed to leap into her throat when she heard his deep, businesslike voice at the other end of the line, and for several seconds she was speechless with nervous tension.

'Are you still there, Melanie?' he demanded abruptly, and the note of authority in his voice seemed to have the desired effect on her vocal cords.

'Yes, I'm ... still here.'

'Good,' he said, and she could visualise him leaning back in his chair with a satisfied look on his hard face. 'I hope you encountered no problems this morning when you handed in your resignation?'

'You saw to it that I wouldn't,' she snapped at him, twisting the cord between her fingers and wishing it was his neck.

'Do I detect a note of anger in your voice?'

'Yes, you do,' she admitted, her hand clenching the receiver so tightly that her fingers ached. 'I'm quite capable of handling my own affairs without your interference, thank you.'

'Your affairs are now mine, Melanie, and that's something you'll have to accept once we're married.'

'We're not married yet!' she exclaimed, his immovable manner adding fuel to the fire that raged through her.

'Melanie!' He said her name sharply, almost like a rebuke, then there was a brief hesitation and his voice was once again matter-of-fact. 'I have to attend a meeting in a few minutes, so let's not waste time. I've made arrangements for us to be married quietly at ten o'clock on Saturday morning in that little church close to your home. My secretary has also made an appointment for you at Loriette's between one and two today, and Madame Loriette knows exactly the kind of wedding dress I have in mind for you.'

'Wedding dress?' she echoed stupidly.

'Did you think I would be satisfied with my bride wearing anything else but the traditional white?' his voice mocked her relentlessly.

'But our marriage isn't ... I mean ...' In her confusion she faltered, unable to continue, and grateful that he could not see her flushed cheeks.

'The reason for our marriage may differ slightly from the conventional, but it will be a marriage like every other marriage. I made that quite clear before, didn't I?'

The reminder was unnecessary, and somehow brutal, making it painfully clear that she could expect no mercy from him once he had made her his wife. He would take what he considered just compensation for his leniency, and quite without regard for her feelings.

'Didn't I, Melanie?' Jason demanded harshly, breaking the strained silence between them.

'Yes, you did,' she admitted, determined now never to let him guess how much she feared him.

'Anything else?'

'Yes,' Melanie replied with a flash of spirit. 'If I must wear white, then I would prefer to purchase the dress somewhere less expensive than Loriette's.'

'You'll do as I say, and don't let the cost concern you.'

'I can't afford——'

'I *can* afford it.'

Melanie sucked her breath in sharply. 'You mean you're going to pay for it?'

'Yes.'

Incredulity and anger washed over her. 'And if I don't want to accept your generosity?'

'For your grandmother's sake, you will,' he assured her with infuriating confidence.

She was speechless for a few seconds as she digested his statement, her heart thudding anxiously at the ruthless determination in his voice, and feeling a little sick as she realised, not for the first time, that he had the whip hand.

'I think I'm beginning to hate you,' she told him, her voice shaking with suppressed anger and helplessness.

'Good,' he replied in his usual abrupt manner. 'I'll call for you at seven this evening and while we're dining together somewhere I'll tell you of the rest of my plans.'

The line went dead before she could reply and she found that she was shaking so much that she could hardly replace the receiver. It was a near impossible task trying to work after that, but she somehow managed to get through the rest of the morning and, despite her reluctance to carry out Jason's instructions, she found herself taking a bus to Madame Loriette's fashion house during her lunch hour.

Madame Loriette, dark-haired, slender, and elegant, surveyed Melanie critically when she arrived, but her tight-lipped expression finally relaxed into a smile that melted some of the coldness about Melanie's heart.

'Mr Kerr should have been in the fashion business,' she announced caustically, 'but I must admit that I find myself agreeing with his choice of style to suit your fairness. I won't be a moment.'

Madame Loriette seemed to float across the carpeted floor of her showroom to disappear behind the heavily draped curtains in the corner, and Melanie was left with the infuriating feeling that she was being treated like a child who had been sent out to select a party dress, only to find that the choice had already been made by a domineering parent prior to her arrival.

'I think you'll like this,' Madame Loriette stated when she returned a few minutes later with the silken folds of a dress draped across her arms. 'If you'll come this way then you could try it on.'

Fighting back her desire to tell Madame Loriette she was wasting her time, Melanie followed her into the cubicle, but as she felt the smoothness of the material against her skin she experienced a feeling of pleasure she could not deny. The style was beautiful in its simplicity, the expensive silk and fine imported lace a perfect foil for her slender, youthful figure. The wide yet modest neckline displayed the graceful curve of her neck and shoulders, while carefully stitched darts accentuated the fulness of her breasts, and Melanie, staring at herself in the mirror, felt as though she were looking at a stranger; a stranger with wide blue eyes darkened by the turbulence of her thoughts. There should have been joy in the selection of her wedding gown, but instead there was a coldness sharpening on a growing fear which she found difficult to ignore.

She met Madame Loriette's questioning glance in the mirror, and managed a smile. 'It's beautiful!'

Madame Loriette nodded with satisfaction, her dark eyes appraising Melanie a little critically. 'It's as if the dress had been made especially for you, my dear, and it isn't difficult to see what it is about you that finally made a man like Jason Kerr lose his heart.'

Melanie did not attempt a reply but, while she was dressing for her dinner appointment with Jason that evening, she recalled Madame Loriette's remark, and could not prevent the bitter laughter that spilled over her lips. Jason Kerr had no heart to lose. His masculine virility demanded the fulfilment of his desires, and circumstances had cruelly made her the object of his desire because of her love for her grandmother and Greystone Manor.

A car came up the drive, its lights making a sweeping arc across the night sky, and Melanie, her amber-coloured chiffon gown swaying about her legs, hurried down the stairs and across the hall to admit Jason. Her heart thudded uncomfortably at his tallness and the breadth of his shoulders in the jacket of his dark evening suit, and she was strangely relieved when he suggested that they leave at once. In the darkness of his car she would at least have some protection from the disturbing quality of his glances.

Jason drove a little way out of the city to a small, quiet restaurant where he knew they could have a little privacy, so he explained to her when she questioned him nervously about the direction he was taking. The owner of the restaurant welcomed Jason like an old friend, and they were shown to a corner table which was set a little apart from the others with a potted palm as added protection from the rest of the diners.

They were served wine which Jason had obviously ordered prior to their arrival, and Melanie sipped at it nervously while he scrutinised the menu and made a selection, but, facing Jason across the small, candlelit table, Melanie promptly lost her appetite, and found herself unable to do justice to the superbly cooked meal. She did little more than rearrange her food on her plate, and although Jason frowned at her once or twice, he finished his meal in silence.

'More wine?' he asked as their plates were cleared away.

'No, thank you.'

He took a slim gold cigarette case from his jacket pocket and opened it. 'Do you mind if I smoke?'

'Please yourself,' she said stiffly.

'It would please me more if you relaxed a little instead of sitting there looking as if you're afraid I might have plans to seduce you in the car on the way home,' he remarked, calmly selecting a cigarette and lighting it.

Melanie wished the floor would give way beneath her, but she was determined not to let him see how much he had embarrassed her as she met his glance squarely and said:

'You don't strike me as the kind of man who would select the interior of a car as a venue for your seduction scenes.'

'You're quite right,' he replied smoothly, his eyes glittering dangerously in the candlelight. 'At my age I prefer a little comfort when seeking that kind of excitement, so you can relax.'

'You surely don't expect me to relax when I'm faced with the prospect of having to marry a complete stranger like yourself, do you?'

'You're a stranger to me too, don't forget,' he reminded her mockingly, 'and although the idea of marriage has never appealed to me, I can't say that I find the idea entirely appalling.'

'For a man it's different,' she argued, unable to hold his glance much longer.

'Is it?'

Melanie's hands clenched and unclenched nervously in her lap. 'You're demanding an awful lot of me, and I—I don't think I can go through with it.'

'Then I take it I must contact my lawyer in the morning and start proceedings for the sale of Greystone Manor?'

'No!' Her lashes flew up swiftly, the look of fear in her eyes giving way to puzzlement. 'You know very well that I want to avoid that at all costs, but if only I could understand your reasoning! Why are you insisting that I should marry you?'

'Would you really like to know?' Jason demanded, his eyes narrowed against the film of smoke rising up from his cigarette.

'Yes . . . yes, I would!'

'Your prim little soul isn't going to like what I have to say,' he warned her, but Melanie believed she was past the stage of being shocked by anything he had to say.

'There's nothing in this entire business that appeals to me,' she said stiffly, 'but tell me the reason nevertheless.'

Jason flicked the ash off his cigarette and leaned towards her across the table, the candlelight giving him a devilish expression that held her fascinated glance without effort as he spoke.

'From the moment I saw you standing beside your father's grave, I wanted you, and when I saw you again later that day I was determined to have you, one way or the other.'

His bald statement had been made quite matter-of-factly, very much as one would remark upon an item in a shop window which one intended to purchase, but it still had the power to shake Melanie considerably, and it was several seconds before she regained her composure enough to speak.

'I don't suppose it's occurred to you that your selfish desire could ruin my entire life?'

'What a typically feminine thought!' he mocked her with a cruel twist of his lips. 'Haven't you realised yet that when our marriage is over and done with, you'll have paid your father's debt in full, and you'll have safeguarded your grandmother's peace of mind?'

'I realise that,' she retorted bitterly, 'but in the process I shall have lost my self-respect.'

'But you'll have gained so much more,' he added softly, and the raw sensuality emanating from his manner and his voice had an almost hypnotic effect on her before she was able to shake herself free.

Jason discussed with her the arrangements he had made, telling her, too, that they would spend a week alone in his chalet in the Drakensberg after their wedding. It sounded desolate and frightening to Melanie, but what frightened her most at that moment was the way her pulses were reacting to his glances.

In a frantic hurry now to get away from this man and the effect he was beginning to have on her, she waited for the opportune moment and said shakily, 'I think I would like to go home now, if you don't mind.'

'As you wish,' he said calmly, getting to his feet and placing her wrap lightly about her shoulders, but as he escorted her from the restaurant she could still feel her skin tingling where his fingers had touched her accidentally.

Neither of them made any attempt at conversation on the way back to Greystone Manor, and Melanie heaved a shuddering sigh of relief when he wished her 'goodnight' at the door, and left without so much as touching her hand.

His action surprised her all the same. For a man who, not an hour ago, had announced cold-bloodedly that he wanted her, he was behaving in an extraordinary manner. Apart from that hateful kiss he had given her in his office a few days ago, and his display of affection in Granny Bridget's company later that same afternoon, he had not touched her unnecessarily. She could not think of anything she wanted less than to be kissed and held by Jason Kerr, but that did not prevent her from being curious about this man she had agreed to marry.

At Granny Bridget's invitation Jason had dinner at their home almost every evening that week, and Melanie saw her grandmother succumb to the charm Jason exuded in her presence. His deception was so faultless that Granny Bridget and Sister Wilson were both too starry-eyed with adoration to notice that Melanie was steadily becoming a shadow of her former happy self.

The arrangements for the wedding were inevitably often discussed, but Melanie seldom participated, brushing off her grandmother's queries by saying she was happy to leave everything in their capable hands.

It was Jason, however, who made most of the arrangements, and Melanie shrank inwardly as the day of their
wedding approached inexorably.

The chill of autumn was in the air when Melanie
stepped out of the office building for the last time that
Friday afternoon, and she hastily fastened the buttons
of her knitted jacket.

'Melanie!'

Her nerves reacted to the sound of that deep voice
and she swung round sharply to see Jason holding open
the rear door of a large white chauffeur-driven Mercedes. She hesitated only briefly before she climbed in
beside him, and the car pulled away smoothly to become a part of the late afternoon exodus from the city.

'I usually prefer driving myself, but my car is in for
a service, and I shan't get it before tomorrow morning,'
Jason told her a little impatiently as he intercepted her
curious glance at the chauffeur.

'I understood that I wouldn't be seeing you this evening,' she said, lowering her voice automatically because
of the uniformed black man in the front seat.

'You understood correctly, but I have something I
would like you to wear tomorrow.'

A small, flat leather case was dropped carelessly into
her lap and, for some unaccountable reason, she was
afraid to touch it.

'Open it,' Jason ordered quietly, and she found herself obeying his command reluctantly.

She managed to undo the old-fashioned catch with
trembling fingers, but caught her breath sharply when
the lid flew open to reveal its priceless contents. Against
the blue velvet backing nestled an exquisitely beautiful
pearl necklace, and even in the shadowy interior of the
car the stones glowed richly.

'It was my mother's,' Jason explained stiffly, and
Melanie's throat tightened.

For the first time since joining him in the back of the Mercedes, she turned in her seat towards him, but her searching, puzzled glance had to be content with his harsh, uncommunicative profile. What was he thinking? she wondered curiously. And what really lay beneath that hard, unbending exterior of his? She studied him intently for a few moments, her glance lingering on the strands of grey hair at his temples, and the way his hair showed a tendency to curl against the back of his strong neck.

He turned his head unexpectedly and, embarrassed at being caught staring, she flushed and looked away, closing the lid of the small leather case with a decisive snap.

'I couldn't possibly wear this necklace,' she said jerkily, placing the case on the seat between them and staring miserably out of the window without noticing that the traffic had thinned out as they turned off on to the road that led to Greystone Manor.

'Why not?' he demanded icily.

'I don't feel that I have the right to wear it,' she explained quietly, clasping her hands tightly in an effort to control their shaking. 'Besides, it's ... it's far too valuable,' she added, filled with anxiety at the thought of something happening to the necklace while it was in her possession, but Jason had no intention of having his wish thwarted, and his hard fingers gripped her chin, forcing her to meet his compelling glance.

'I want you to wear that necklace tomorrow, and that's an order, Melanie.' His fingers tightened their grip painfully. 'If you don't ...'

He left his sentence unfinished, but it had an ominous ring to it that sent a shiver of fear through her, and she found herself agreeing before she could prevent herself.

Jason released her instantly but, to her dismay, he trailed his fingers lightly across her pale cheek and down the column of her throat until she could actually feel her own pulse throbbing against his exploring fingertips. Then his hand clasped her throat, almost as if he wished to choke her, and she raised wide, frightened eyes to his.

'You're being wise to obey me,' he said calmly and, for the second time since knowing him, she felt his hard mouth pressed against her own for a brief moment before he released her and turned away to stare out of the window as if he had abruptly forgotten her existence.

How dared he treat her in this hateful manner? she asked herself fiercely, clenching her fists until her nails bit into her palms, but her jerky pulses told her that she had not been left entirely unaffected by his kiss and her anger mounted against him for some inexplicable reason.

She opened her mouth to say something, but they had already turned into Greystone Manor's drive, and what she had to say would perhaps be better left unsaid in front of Jason's chauffeur, no matter how discreetly he had treated their presence in the back of the Mercedes.

'Get to bed early tonight,' Jason said as he left her on the patio, and Melanie did not wait to see the car go down the drive before entering the house.

After dinner that evening an uncommon tiredness made her refuse the sleeping tablet Sister Wilson offered her, but she regretted her hasty refusal when, after sleeping for no longer than an hour, she found herself tossing in her bed from eleven o'clock onwards. Not wanting to wake Sister Wilson, she went quietly down to the kitchen and warmed herself a glass of milk, but it lacked the desired effect, and she finally gave up the struggle to spend the night pacing her bedroom floor.

Within a few hours it would be daylight, and the moment she had silently dreaded all week would be upon her. She could no longer thrust aside her fears, nor did she dare dwell on them. The thought of marrying Jason Kerr, of being possessed by this ruthless, arrogant man, was enough to send her running panic-stricken to her grandmother's room to confess the truth, and this she dared not do. Jason had made it possible for them to keep their home for a time, and she would have to fulfil her side of the bargain, no matter how much she hated it.

In the grey light of dawn, she crawled into bed and sheer exhaustion made her fall asleep to be awakened two hours later by Sister Wilson, looking bright and cheerful as she carried in a breakfast tray.

'It's the bride's privilege to have breakfast in bed on her wedding day,' she announced, placing the tray on Melanie's lap. 'It's going to be the happiest day of your life.'

'It's going to be the most dreaded day of my life,' Melanie corrected silently as she smiled her thanks and waited for the door to close behind Sister Wilson's uniformed figure before she made an effort to eat something, but the food choked her, and tears threatened as she pushed aside the tray and went through to the bathroom to run her bath water.

An hour later, and dressed in Madame Loriette's creation, she stood staring at herself in the full-length mirror. 'This *must* be a nightmare,' she thought frantically. 'I *can't* marry Jason. I don't love him. I don't even *like* him—I despise him!'

That was not quite true either. She was undeniably fascinated by him, and she would have had to be blind not to notice that he was extremely attractive despite the harshness of his hawk-like features. She recalled the pressure of his lips against her own, and trembled.

Would it be so bad to have him make love to her? she wondered a little breathlessly.

A knock at her door brought her to her senses, and Flora stepped into the room, her dark eyes gleaming with admiration as she stared for a moment at Melanie, then she remembered the reason for her call.

'Telephone for you, Miss Melanie,' she said, plugging in the instrument beside the bed and hurrying out before Melanie could thank her.

With the absurd wish that it would be Jason, she lifted the receiver, but the voice that came over the line was decidedly feminine, and well-modulated. She introduced herself as Delia Cummings, and Melanie frowned as she tried to recall where she had heard that name before.

'I realise that this is your wedding day,' the woman said, 'but I felt you ought to know exactly where you stand as far as Jason is concerned.'

'Miss Cummings, I——'

'He's mine!' that beautiful voice announced huskily without giving Melanie an opportunity to speak. 'He's had his little affairs in the past, but he has always returned to me in the end.'

Melanie felt very much like saying, 'You're welcome to him this minute,' but she controlled her wayward tongue and instead said calmly,

'Marriage is a little more binding than a casual affair, don't you think?'

Delia Cummings laughed unpleasantly. 'Jason has never had any respect for the marriage vows. He's a law unto himself, and when he tires of you he'll be back where he belongs—with me!'

'I wouldn't be too sure of that if I were you,' Melanie could not help saying.

'I *am* sure, darling,' Delia Cummings replied with astounding confidence. 'A leopard never changes its spots, if you'll forgive the old cliché, so you might as well heed my warning. 'Bye, darling, and *do* enjoy your wedding. The memory will be all you'll have left in time.'

The line went dead, and Melanie replaced the receiver slowly, aware that, for some inexplicable reason, Delia Cummings had succeeded in hurting her.

CHAPTER FOUR

STANDING beside Jason in the small stone church not far from Greystone Manor, Melanie felt curiously detached from the proceedings. Tall, wide-shouldered, and immaculate in a dark suit and striped tie, Jason was a formidable stranger, his face an impenetrable mask as he placed the circle of gold on her finger to symbolise the fact that she had now become his wife.

His wife!

'Dear God, this can't be real!' she thought in a moment of panic, but it was as real as the confetti which was showered on them some minutes later as they stepped out into the sunshine. A little more than half a dozen people, of whom Melanie knew only Granny Bridget and Sister Wilson, crowded around them to wish them well, but an ingenious newspaper photographer had somehow discovered their plans, and his camera flashed several times before he sprinted towards his car and drove off. The incident had occurred so quickly and unexpectedly that it was over before Melanie realised what had taken place and, taking her cue from Jason, she behaved as though nothing had happened.

They were driven back to Greystone Manor where they drank champagne on the terrace, and somehow Melanie drifted through it all in a state of unnatural calmness which was disturbed, only briefly, when the time came to say goodbye to her grandmother. Jason, however, took firm command of the situation, and Melanie found herself whisked off to the silver-grey Jaguar parked in the driveway before there was time for an emotional scene to erupt.

'Now we can relax,' Jason remarked casually when they finally turned on to the N3 to Heidelberg, and Melanie almost laughed out loud.

She could not recall when last she had been able to relax and, judging by the tension which seemed to grip every muscle in her body, it would be a long time before she would be able to do as Jason suggested. They were heading for his chalet in the picturesque and mountainous Drakensberg, but to Melanie it felt as though she were being taken to a prison.

'How long will it take us to get to your chalet?' she asked as the silence threatened to become uncomfortable between them.

'Four to five hours if we don't stop too often along the way. I would like to get there before dark,' he added frowningly without taking his eyes off the ribbon of road ahead. 'The mountain road can be treacherous after sunset.'

Melanie did not question this and lapsed into silence, her thoughts whirling in uncomfortable circles as she tried to visualise spending a week in the mountains with Jason. They would be alone together, and nothing appealed to her less than to have to spend several days alone in the company of a man who, for some obscure reason, always succeeded in making her feel nervous and edgy.

She glanced his way unobtrusively and tried to tell herself that she had nothing to fear but, as her insides twisted themselves into a tighter knot, she knew that she had failed miserably. His hands were resting on the steering wheel in a relaxed manner, but they were nevertheless in complete control of the powerful Jaguar as it sped southwards across the country.

Her fascinated glance lingered on his hands, and she

noticed for the first time the well-kept fingernails. His hands were strong and capable-looking, and they were hands that could crush as well as caress with equally devastating effects.

Startled by the trend of her thoughts, Melanie looked away hastily and stared blindly ahead of her. Why should the mere idea of being caressed by Jason disturb her so? she wondered as she tried to control the rapid beating of her heart. She hardly knew him, and she despised him for forcing her into this loveless marriage. Why then should the thought of his hands caressing her send the blood flowing more swiftly through her veins?

'This is ridiculous,' she rebuked herself silently. 'I'm tired and overwrought, and allowing my imagination to get the better of me.'

She concentrated fiercely on the scenery, and noticed the early signs of the approaching winter. The trees were beginning to shed their leaves, and Melanie watched ruefully as a miniature whirlwind disturbed the carpet of gold beside the road. It swept the leaves high into the air, scattering them in all directions, and carrying some of them several kilometres away before depositing them in the bushy veld where the cattle grazed in a leisurely, undisturbed fashion.

They stopped for lunch at Heidelberg, a beautiful town nestling among the hills, and Melanie was tempted to ask Jason if they could remain there a while longer but, knowing his desire to reach the Drakensberg before dark, she relinquished the idea and waited quietly for him to remove his jacket and tie before getting into the car once more.

'Why don't you lie back and try to sleep?' Jason suggested as they left the town behind them. 'There's a long stretch of uninteresting road ahead before we reach our destination.'

'I'm not sleepy.'

'Please yourself,' he shrugged, and a stony silence settled between them which Melanie did not dare interrupt.

Despite her intention to stay awake, the monotony of the road and the soothing hum of the car's engine began to have a relaxing effect on her. She was tired, desperately tired, and leaning back against the headrest, she felt her eyelids drooping as if they were filled with lead. For a time she drifted on a plane of awareness, fighting against the desire to sleep, but she finally gave up the subconscious struggle and slipped into a dreamless sleep from which she did not awaken for some considerable time.

'Where are we?' she asked eventually, rousing herself and blinking at the swiftly setting sun as Jason turned off the tarred highway on to a gravel road.

'We left Harrismith behind us some time ago,' he replied as the car gathered speed. 'We should reach our destination in less than an hour.'

'Good heavens! I must have slept for *hours*,' she exclaimed, brushing her hair out of her eyes and straightening her skirt which, to her embarrassment, had managed to shift higher to expose her shapely knees.

Her action did not go unnoticed, and as Jason glanced at her briefly she caught a hint of amusement in his eyes before he concentrated on the road once more, but that look had been enough to send the colour surging into her cheeks.

'You can't see much of the mountains in this light,' he said easily, 'but you'll see them at their best in the morning.'

In the morning! Oh, if only it were morning already and this dreaded night were over, she thought, anxiety chilling her to the marrow at the prospect of what was yet to come.

The minutes sped by relentlessly, and the road inevitably began to twist and turn precariously along the edge of the mountain. Melanie held her breath, but Jason seemed to be well acquainted with the route they were taking, and he looked quite relaxed as he negotiated the hairpin bends in the road.

Surely they could not go much higher, she thought as Jason manoeuvred the car round yet another sharp bend, and then everything seemed to happen at once. A rockfall had created an impassable barrier across the road, and in the fast gathering dusk they were almost on top of it before the headlights illuminated the obstruction.

'Jason, look out!' she cried unnecessarily, for Jason had already swerved the car violently to the right and away from the sheer drop on the left, at the same time slamming his foot on to the brake, bringing the car to a slithering stop, and only just preventing it from careering into the ditch.

'Damn!' he muttered angrily, applying the handbrake and switching off the engine. 'Are you all right?'

'Yes—yes, I'm fine,' she gasped, staring up into his anxious face and shaken by the knowledge that only her seatbelt had saved her from crashing through the windscreen.

His hand touched her cold cheek briefly before he undid his own seatbelt and climbed out. The cold air swept into the car and Melanie shivered as she followed his example without hesitation, almost as if she were afraid to remain in the car without him.

'Does this sort of thing happen often?' she asked as she stood beside him surveying the mountain of rocks strewn across the road.

'Not to my knowledge it doesn't.'

Melanie wrapped her arms about herself as the cold penetrated her blue linen suit. 'What are we going to do?'

'There are two possibilities.' He rubbed his chin

thoughtfully. 'I could remove just enough of these rocks in order to get the car through, or——'

'That would be too risky,' she interrupted, amazed that he could even consider something so dangerous. 'The soil doesn't seem to be very firm close to the edge of the road, and it would never take the weight of the car.'

Thinking that she was concerned for her own safety, he said harshly, 'I wasn't suggesting that you should be in the car with me when I attempt it.'

'It makes no difference whether I'm with you or not,' she argued hotly. 'I still think it's too much of a risk.'

He stared at her for a moment, his grey eyes glittering strangely in the semi-darkness. 'You obviously haven't considered the possibility that you'll be free if I should plunge to my death over the edge.'

'I wouldn't want my freedom at the expense of your death, thank you,' she said coldly, not certain whether she was shaking as a result of the chill in the air, or the frightening thought that someone as vitally alive as Jason should be crushed to death in the wreckage of his car. 'What's the other alternative?' she asked, managing to control the tremor in her voice.

Jason drew her away from the edge of the road towards the car. 'It will take the best part of two hours to remove this lot, but it's something that will have to wait for morning. There's usually a drastic drop in temperature after sunset here in the Drakensberg, so the only other alternative is to leave the car here and walk the rest of the way.'

'Is it far?'

'Not if we take a short cut along the path over this hill,' Jason said abruptly as he pulled on his jacket and took the keys to unlock the boot. 'We'll take a few of the small things with us, and I'll come back later for the suitcases.'

Melanie had fortunately had the good sense to throw

in her coat at the last minute, for her teeth were chattering as Jason helped her into it. Ten minutes later, carrying nothing more than her handbag and vanity case, she was still stumbling after him with the beam of the torch he carried guiding her steps, but dry twigs had ripped her stockings, and she was certain that her high-heeled shoes were ruined beyond repair.

'Jason, could ... could we stop for a moment?' she gasped, almost succeeding in twisting her ankle on the uneven ground.

'Tired?' he asked abruptly, indicating with the torch that she should sit down on the large boulder beside the path.

'A little out of breath,' she admitted, taking the weight off her feet and wriggling her left foot slightly to test her ankle.

Jason dropped his haversack on to the ground, and sat down beside her to light a cigarette. He had switched off the torch to save the batteries, and in the darkness she was suddenly intensely aware of his nearness, of the muscular thigh pressed against her own, and the arm he had placed almost protectively about her.

'I'm sorry about this.'

'It's not your fault,' she protested hastily, a little flustered by his unexpected apology, and the cloak of intimacy provided by the velvety darkness of the star-studded night. 'If I'd known, though, that we'd end our journey with a cross-country hike, I would have dressed myself more appropriately, then I might have enjoyed it more.'

'Do you enjoy trudging through the countryside?'

'I thought you said you knew so much about me,' she laughed nervously, and when he did not reply, she said: 'I do enjoy walking in the country, but I don't often have the opportunity to indulge in that sort of pastime.'

'You'll be able to do a lot of walking while we're here,' he said without the usual hint of mockery in his voice, and Melanie wished suddenly that she could see his face.

'Do we have much further to go?' she asked at length when she could no longer bear his disturbing nearness and the strange effect it had on her pulse rate.

'Another five minutes and we should be there.'

'Then let's go on,' she suggested, escaping the circle of his arm and fumbling in the darkness for her hand-bag and vanity case.

Jason crushed the stub of his cigarette beneath his heel and switched on the torch. They walked the rest of the way in silence, and as the ground levelled out she caught a glimpse of the chalet silhouetted against the night sky.

It was difficult to see much of it in the darkness, but the beam of the torch played briefly across face-bricks and solid wood as Jason inserted the key in the lock and pushed open the door. Melanie followed him inside a little gingerly, but instead of encountering the musti-ness of a place not often used, she found the air fresh as though the room had been aired recently.

'Confound it! The generator hasn't been switched on,' Jason stated irritably as he flicked a few switches in what appeared to be the lounge. 'Are you afraid of the dark?'

Her heart pounded uncomfortably. 'N-not really ... why?'

He gestured with the torch. 'I'll have to take this with me in order to see what I'm doing. Here,' he thrust a packet of matches into her cold hand. 'Light the fire while I'm out and get yourself warm.'

He strode from the room and out the front door, his footsteps crunching on the gravel outside, but a few seconds later she could hear nothing except a deafening silence which was broken only by the chirping of a cricket in the undergrowth outside. The inky blackness was somehow frightening, and her hands shook as she struck a match and lit the fire in the hearth. The newspapers and dry twigs caught alight swiftly, heating the carefully packed logs, and illuminating the room considerably.

Kneeling down to warm her hands, Melanie glanced about her, taking in the sturdy wooden furniture and the brightly coloured seat cushions. There was nothing elaborate about the furnishings, but everything was entirely masculine and, if it had not been for the rings glittering on the third finger of her left hand, she would have felt that she was trespassing on a domain built to the exclusion of women.

The faint sound of a motor starting up reached her ears, and seconds later the lights flickered on, hurting her eyes after the accustomed darkness. Jason returned moments later and Melanie rose stiffly in front of the fire as he approached her.

'I'll go down to the car and collect the rest of our things. Will you be all right on your own?'

The thought of him going back all that way to the car now seemed like sheer lunacy. She had felt the draught of icy air when he had come in from starting the generator, and nothing, not even her fear of him, would induce her to step outside again.

'You can't go out again. It must be freezing outside.'

'Our suitcases are still in the car,' he reminded her grimly, turning up the collar of his jacket.

'I dare say we'll manage somehow.'

Too late she realised the implication of her hasty words, and her glance fell before his.

'*I'll* manage , but I don't think you'll enjoy sleeping in the raw,' he mocked her mercilessly, taking in her flushed cheeks and quivering lips before he muttered something unintelligible and turned away. 'I suggest you see what you can find in the kitchen for us to eat while I'm out.'

The front door slammed behind him seconds later, and Melanie found herself alone once more with nothing but a desolate silence for company. Taking off her coat, she threw it over the back of a chair and, glancing down at her damaged stockings, she grimaced and peeled them off, pushing them into the pocket of her coat before she began to explore the chalet.

There were two bedrooms, both modestly furnished, and each with their own private bathroom, but the large double bed in the one room sent a quiver of apprehension through her that made her retreat swiftly. There was no real way of escape from this situation for her. The door of the steel cage had snapped shut and she was a prisoner at the mercy of the man she had married that morning.

Brushing aside her unpleasant thoughts, she explored further and, to her delight, she discovered that the kitchen was surprisingly modern, with cupboards stocked with tinned food, and an electric oven. A puzzled frown creased her brow when she found that someone had thoughtfully started up the paraffin refrigerator prior to their arrival, but she was even more startled when she discovered it was stocked up with everything they could possibly require, from fresh meat to crispy vegetables. A friendly neighbour, perhaps? she wondered as she took out a packet of steak and a container of eggs.

Jason would have to be satisfied with an omelette and steak, she decided, and just to set it off, she would open up one of the small tins of mushrooms she had seen in one of the cupboards.

Engrossed in what she was doing, she found the time flew past and she looked up with an uncomfortable start of surprise when she heard the front door open and close. She heard Jason's footsteps echoing down the passage and the sound of suitcases being dropped on to the floor, and then he was entering the kitchen, coming up behind her as she dished the food into their plates.

'Hm ...' he sniffed appreciatively. 'Being out in the cold has given me an appetite.'

'I thought we could eat in front of the fire,' she said hesitantly, not knowing him well enough to decide whether he would approve or not.

'Sounds fine to me,' he smiled briefly, thrusting his hands into his pockets and standing aside while she put their plates on the tray along with the knives and forks. 'Need any help?'

She shot him a surprised glance and said, half in jest, and half in earnest, 'You can take the tray through, if you like.'

Never for one moment did she suspect that he would do exactly as she had suggested, and she found herself following him through to the lounge in an astonished silence. He placed the tray on a low table close to the fire and left the room, only to return seconds later with a bottle of champagne and two glasses. The cork popped loudly and somehow Melanie found herself standing facing him with a glass of sparkling champagne in her trembling hand.

'To us,' he said, touching the rim of his glass to hers, then he raised it to his lips, and she followed his example, unable to find her voice to echo his toast.

Her glance went beyond him and she gasped audibly as she saw for the first time the mounted head of a lion above the stone fireplace, its eyes gleaming maliciously, and its fangs bared ready for the kill. It looked very much alive, and she thanked heaven that she had been unaware of its existence while she had waited around in the darkness for Jason to return. She shivered involuntarily, and Jason's amused glance followed hers.

'A farmer in the eastern Transvaal was having problems with a marauding lion some years ago,' he explained as they sat down to start their meal. 'I was part of the team that went in search of it.'

'Did you kill it? Is that why you had its head mounted?'

'I killed it,' he said with a sort of flat finality in his voice that prevented her from asking further questions.

She tried to eat, but her glance kept returning to the silent, snarling animal above the fireplace, and the steak she had taken such pains to prepare turned to sawdust in her mouth.

After two glasses of champagne, and very little to eat, she felt lightheaded, and slightly more courageous, as Jason leaned back against the cushions on the bench and stretched his long legs towards the log fire.

'That was good,' he murmured, closing his eyes and smiling faintly.

She studied him in silence for a moment, wondering just what he was thinking, but her own wild thoughts intruded, and she quickly gathered up the dishes to take them through to the kitchen.

'I'll make us something to drink.'

'Make mine coffee,' he said without opening his eyes. 'Strong, black, and without sugar.'

Melanie washed the dishes while she waited for the kettle to boil, and the kitchen was as tidy as she had found it originally when she returned to the lounge with their coffee.

The silence between them was unnerving, and Melanie's courage deserted her as she became aware of Jason observing her much in the same way as that animal above the fireplace must have observed its prey before attacking and, like that beast of prey, Jason could afford to be smugly patient. His prey was cornered, and there to be taken at his leisure.

Her nerve ends quivered in protest, and after a desperate search for something to say that would alleviate the tension, she asked, 'Do you come here often?'

'As often as I can when I need to get away from the pressure of work. It's peaceful and quiet, and the nearest telephone is five kilometres away.'

She wondered suddenly whether he had ever brought Delia Cummings to his chalet, but she discarded the thought distastefully and asked instead, 'Who stocked up the cupboards and lit the paraffin refrigerator?'

'I've got someone in Bergville who usually takes care of these things for me.'

There was a hint of impatience in his voice, and she had the feeling that his muscles were tensed, ready to leap. Her supposition was so strong that she had jumped to her feet before she was able to prevent herself and, realising how foolish she must appear, she asked him for his empty cup in order to escape from his alarming presence for a few minutes.

Jason calmly held out his cup and she took an involuntary step forward, realising too late how easily she had walked into the trap when his free hand shot out and gripped her wrist. She was dragged down into his arms, and fear clutched at her throat, making it impossible to speak as she found herself staring up into his darkly tanned face.

'You're afraid of me, aren't you?'

It was a statement, not a question, and his perceptiveness startled her into an admission. 'Yes, I am.'

'Of me, or of sex in general?'

'A little of both, I think,' she admitted, unable to avoid his penetrating glance.

'Do you consider me to be some sort of monster?'

'No.'

Melanie moistened her dry lips with the tip of her

tongue, completely unaware of the sensuality in that innocent gesture, and her blue glance registered alarm when his eyes darkened with unmistakable desire.

'I don't intend to hurt you unnecessarily, Melanie, but I won't allow you to back out of our agreement.'

His kiss was like a searing, passionate flame that threatened to devour her. She tried to respond, but felt herself go rigid instead in the face of such overwhelming desire. Submerged in a wall of panic, she struggled against him, but her hands encountered hard, unyielding muscles, she knew the futility of her puny efforts.

'For God's sake, Melanie, relax!' he groaned eventually when his caresses, intended to arouse her, merely succeeded in increasing her tenseness.

'I c-can't!' she gasped, humiliatingly close to tears and, more than anything else, wishing herself back in the safety of her own room at Greystone Manor.

Jason's tight-lipped expression chilled her, his fingers biting into the soft flesh of her upper arms as he set her aside firmly and got to his feet. The silence was explosive as he towered over her menacingly, and she shrank back against the cushions, labouring under a feeling of guilt as she waited for him to say something —anything!—that would relieve the electrifying tension in the air.

'I've certainly picked a loser this time,' he said at last, his deep voice grating harshly along her sensitive nerves. 'If there's anything I can't stand, then it's a frigid woman, and God only knows what I saw in you. You're a fake, Melanie; a fake and a fraud. You got what you wanted, but you're not prepared to give anything in return.'

His words cut her to the core and, shaking in every limb, she rose to her feet, determined to disprove his opinion of her in some way.

'Jason ...'

'Please!' He held up his hands in a silencing gesture. 'Whatever it is you may have to say, I'm certain it would be of no interest to me at all, but you needn't be concerned that I shall go back on my word. Your grandmother shall have Greystone Manor for as long as she lives, but as for our marriage, it no longer exists. We'll remain here for a week, as planned, but once we've returned to Johannesburg I shall continue to live my life as before. In the eyes of the law you will be my wife, but don't expect any consideration from me. I shall seek my pleasures elsewhere, regardless of what you, and others, may think.' His eyes, like slivers of ice, raked her from head to foot with a degrading insolence that drove every scrap of blood from her face. 'Have I made myself clear?'

Her lips moved but no sound came, and she nodded mutely instead, the subdued light in the room casting deep shadows beneath eyes that held a wounded expression.

'The first room down the passage is yours,' he said coldly as he turned his back on her and stared into the remains of the fire. 'Go to bed—and don't bother locking the door,' he added cynically. 'You're quite safe.'

Her trembling legs carried her from his presence, but as the bedroom door closed behind her, she felt something snap inside her, and the weeks of sorrow and tension took their toll. Sinking to the floor beside the bed, she buried her face in her arms, and wept long and bitter tears until she felt sure that not a shred of emotion remained within her.

'You're a fake and a fraud,' she recalled Jason's stinging remark some time later when she lay curled up in the large double bed wondering how she was going to cope with this new situation. 'You're more than a fake and a fraud,' she told herself after some deliberation. 'You're a coward! The worst kind of coward!'

Melanie awoke the following morning with the sun streaming in through the window. She stretched and yawned, trying to remember when last she had slept so soundly, and then she realised suddenly where she was ... and why! This was supposed to have been their honeymoon, and Jason had fully intended that it should be, but things had worked out differently. She had spent the night alone in the large bed, and Jason, she supposed, had spent it in the spare room further down the passage.

It was after eight, she realised with some surprise as she sat up in bed and glanced at her wristwatch. Was Jason still asleep? she wondered as she became aware of the silence in the chalet, then she noticed the folded sheet of white notepaper which had obviously been pushed beneath her door. Hurrying barefooted across the carpeted floor, she picked up the note and unfolded it.

'I'm taking a stroll down to the car to see what can be done about removing the rocks. Don't expect me back before eleven. Jason.'

Melanie read it through once more, a smile lifting the corners of her mouth as she stared at his bold handwriting. After all the angry words he had flung at her last night, stating that she should not expect any consideration from him, it was quite surprising that he should have been considerate enough to leave her this note telling her where he was, and her heart lifted inexplicably.

Bathed and changed into a pair of faded denims, check shirt and sturdy shoes, she made up the bed and went through to the kitchen. There was no sign that Jason had made himself anything to eat before going out and, making up her mind quickly, she searched the refrigerator and found a packet of cold ham. A half hour later, armed with a basket in which she had packed a flask of coffee, cups and sandwiches, she closed the chalet door behind her and strode out in the direction they had come the previous evening.

In the daylight, and wearing suitable shoes, it took her a little more than ten minutes to reach her destination, but she hesitated with uncertainty when she caught sight of Jason just below her. In tight-fitting black slacks and shirtless, with his tanned, muscular torso rippling as he worked, he presented a different picture entirely from the formidable business executive she had come to know, and she wondered nervously how he would react to her presence after last night. Would he send her away in anger, or would he treat her with cold indifference?

'Well, there's only one way to find out,' she told herself firmly, and, taking a deep breath of fresh mountain air to steady herself, she covered the remainder of the distance swiftly and dropped lightly on to the road beside him.

'Good morning, Jason,' she said quietly, and he dropped the rocks he held in his hands and turned to stare at her, his eyes narrowed against the sun, and his face expressionless.

'You didn't have anything to eat this morning,' she tried again when he continued to stare at her in silence. 'I thought I'd come down here and share my breakfast with you.'

For several nerve-racking seconds he continued to say nothing, then he nodded abruptly and gestured towards the grass verge beside the road where the shade of an acacia tree offered them sufficient protection from the stinging rays of the sun. They sat down with the basket between them and, while Jason helped himself to a sandwich, Melanie poured their coffee.

They ate their breakfast to the sound of birds chattering in the trees, and with the vista of ruggedly beautiful mountain peaks all around them. A scavenger hawk circled lazily against the backdrop of the cloudless blue sky, and Melanie watched it for some time before some sixth sense warned her that she was being observed.

Turning her head slowly, she met Jason's steady regard, and deep within her something stirred, an awareness so fleeting that it was gone before she could grasp it.

Unable to look away, she sustained his glance and withstood the searching scrutiny of those steel-grey eyes. She was aware of the same breathless feeling which she had encountered at their first meeting and, puzzled, she finally looked away, focusing her attention on a beetle scurrying into the bushes.

'What was this all in aid of, Melanie?'

The sound of his voice startled her and, lowering her gaze to her tightly clenched hands in her lap, she said slowly, 'Perhaps it's just my way of saying ... I'm sorry I was such a coward last night.'

Jason was silent and, stealing a glance at him, she saw that he was staring at her thoughtfully as if he were digesting her apology and assessing its worth.

'I accept that,' he said at length, gesturing vaguely with his hands, 'but where do we go from here?'

Determined to prove him wrong in his assessment of her character, she said quite clearly, 'I mean to fulfil my obligations, Jason, but ...' She faltered, and swallowed nervously before continuing. 'I need a little time. I— I can't just——'

'Get into bed with a comparative stranger, even though he does happen to be your husband?' he filled in for her questioningly, and as she nodded, her cheeks flaming with embarrassment, he laughed harshly. 'All right, I'll give you time to adjust, and in the meantime we'll just allow nature to take its course.'

The basket was removed, and the distance between them lessened until she felt his thigh pressing hard against her own. Her nervous glance took in the wide expanse of his hair-roughened chest, the strong column of his throat, and the slightly sardonic expression on his face as his hand gripped her shoulder, forcing her back against the softness of the wild grass that grew high up on the mountains. His wide shoulders were like wings spread out above her, blotting out the sky, and making her aware of her own frailty in the face of such over-powering masculinity. The birds in the trees ceased their chattering, or was it perhaps that her heart was pounding so loudly that it drowned out all other sounds? she wondered distractedly.

'Jason?'

'In this game kisses and a little light lovemaking have to be permitted,' he explained mockingly. 'It's called physical contact, and right now I'm in need of it.'

His arms were beneath her, cradling her against the hard warmth of his body while he kissed her sensually and lingeringly, until her body tingled with sensations that left her trembling and breathless when he finally released her and drew her to her feet.

'That was very nice, but there's work to be done,' he said abruptly, and she was left feeling curiously bereft when he turned his back on her and resumed the task of clearing the road.

She offered her help, but it was promptly rejected and, swallowing down her disappointment, she returned to the chalet to occupy herself with airing and tidying the rooms until Jason returned.

CHAPTER FIVE

THE sun was a red ball of fire sinking in the west, changing the appearance of the rugged mountain peaks from drab grey to gold, and finally red.

Melanie sighed audibly, thrusting her hands deeper into the pockets of her parka as the darkness descended on the scene before her. She did not think she would ever tire of watching the magical rays of the setting sun as it transformed the mountains into something so indescribably beautiful that she was always filled with a sense of loss when the moment had passed. If only she was able to grasp that moment of splendour and hold it for a little longer! she thought whimsically.

She had felt like that often during the past few days. Her growing awareness of Jason, and the confusing emotions he awakened in her, resembled her feelings when watching the sunset. Before she could grasp the answer to it all, the moment would be gone, and she would be left feeling more confused than ever before.

They had spent hours together exploring the mountains, and she had discovered, too, that they were not as isolated as she had thought initially, for, less than a kilometre away, there was a group of similar chalets nestled together among the trees. During the bitterly cold evenings they had sat in front of the fire, and she had spent the time pondering the circumstances which had led to their marriage, and the peculiar relationship which now existed between Jason and herself. There were occasions when he had kissed her with a lingering passion, but she had sensed the anger in him when he had thrust her away to resume his cold and distant attitude.

He was, she realised, displaying remarkable control for a man who was accustomed to having his way with women and, although she appreciated the effort he was making, she could not help wondering if she would not still regret the request she had made for time. A man as virile as Jason could not live for lengthy periods without a woman—she did not need much experience to realise that—and Delia Cummings' prediction might yet come true. Jason might get tired of waiting, and turn to Delia instead to resume their affair.

It was a sobering thought, and one which disturbed her more than she cared to realise. It was really no concern of hers how Jason chose to continue living his life, and yet . . . !

Melanie shook herself mentally and went in out of the cold, but, as she packed her suitcase that evening before going to bed, these thoughts returned, and they remained stubbornly until she finally drifted off into an uneasy sleep.

'Well,' said Jason, his voice thick with sarcasm as they drove away from the chalet the following morning, 'the honeymoon is over.'

Melanie bit back a sharp retort, preferring to ignore his remark for the time being as he negotiated the sharp bends in the road. This was not the time nor the place for a confrontation, and it would have to keep until they were home.

Home! Where *was* home? she wondered suddenly, realising that she had no idea whether Jason had a house somewhere outside Johannesburg, or an apartment in the city in order to be near his work.

'Where are we going to live?' she asked, unable to restrain her curiosity a moment longer.

'At my flat,' he said abruptly, obviously in no mood

to enlighten her further, and one glance at his stern profile was enough to make her realise that it would be safer to shelve her questions for the moment.

His apartment, she discovered some hours later, turned out to be a two-bedroomed penthouse with a study, living-room, dining-room, and modern kitchen. It was tastefully and luxuriously furnished in cream and gold, but it sadly lacked that homely, lived-in feeling so evident at Greystone Manor, and Melanie was suddenly indescribably homesick.

Jason carried her suitcase into the main bedroom, and her glance skimmed uncomfortably over the large double bed with its white padded headboard. This was to be her room, she gathered, and it would eventually be the room she shared with Jason. She trembled at the thought, and the tense little silence was broken as Jason gestured abruptly in the direction of the suitcases placed in a row beneath the window.

'I arranged for the remainder of your possessions to be brought here while we were away.'

'Thank you.'

His cool glance swept over her before he turned away and went further down the passage towards the other bedroom, and Melanie sighed with relief as she walked across to the window to draw aside the curtains. It was a peculiar feeling to be staring out across the city with its tall buildings, and the inevitable layers of smog above the skyline. It was such a vastly different sight from the view she had from her bedroom at Greystone Manor that she felt almost physically sick. She opened the window to let in some air, and was thankful at least that the sound of the traffic was muted.

She inspected the wardrobes and then dragged her suitcases closer to start unpacking. She had unpacked two of them and was undoing the catches of the third when she became aware of Jason leaning against the door frame with his thumbs hooked into the belt of his pants. He had exchanged his thick woollen sweater for a blue shirt and dark grey jacket, she noticed at once, and a faint suspicion stirred within her.

'Are you going out?'

He pushed himself away from the door and strolled towards the bed in a leisurely fashion. 'I'm going down to the office, and I doubt if I'll be back before late this evening.'

As he spoke he picked up a silky pink nightdress which she had left lying across the foot of the bed, and she watched in fascinated horror as he held it up to inspect it before his eyes slid down the length of her, almost as if he were trying to imagine her wearing it. A faint smile curled about his mouth as though he had found his mental image of her pleasing, and Melanie felt the air being drained slowly from her lungs.

'Shall I keep your—your dinner in the oven for you?' she managed haltingly, her cheeks suffused with colour as he pulled the nightdress lightly through his fingers before replacing it where he had found it.

'Don't trouble yourself. I'll get something to eat while I'm out. Oh, and ...' his expression was faintly sardonic as he halted halfway towards the door and turned to face her, 'I would appreciate it if you would make up the bed in the spare room for me. You'll find clean linen in the cupboard at the end of the passage.'

He turned on his heel and left, and seconds later she heard the outer door slamming behind him. Only then did her pulse resume its normal pace and, picking up the offending garment, she flung it into the farthest corner of the wardrobe before she resumed her unpacking with renewed energy born of embarrassment and anger.

She discovered later that the room Jason would be occupying was across the passage from the guest bathroom, and it was a room which was just as spacious as her own. The furnishings were similar as well, except for the twin beds which stood against the opposite wall with a glass-topped table between them, and she felt Jason's recent presence so strongly that she almost fled without putting clean linen on the bed as he had instructed.

With Jason out of the way, she explored the spacious penthouse at her leisure. His study, lined with books on engineering and a vast number of other subjects, differed strongly from her father's study at Greystone Manor. Jason's desk was uncluttered, the blotter clean and smooth, and Melanie stared at it thoughtfully. Jason was either meticulously neat, or, like the rest of the penthouse, the study was seldom used. Apart from the rows of books in the shelves there was nothing to give her an insight into the character of the man she had married, and no items, such as objects bought and kept for sentimental reasons, stood about the place. The walls were bare except for two rifles mounted above the ornamental fireplace, and she wondered curiously, but thankfully, why he had taken the mounted head of that ferocious-looking lion to his chalet in the Drakensberg instead of keeping it here in his study.

Melanie shivered and walked across to the telephone on the desk to dial Greystone Manor's number. Sister Wilson answered it almost immediately and, after Melanie had enquired after Granny Bridget's health, they chatted for a few minutes before Melanie rang off with the promise to pay them a visit the following morning.

Further explorations took her through the sliding glass doors leading off the living-room on to the roof garden with its potted shrubs and deck chairs. It could never compare with a real garden, but the greenness of the shrubs relieved the drab greyness of the buildings in the background, and this was something to be thankful for, she decided as she lowered herself on to the recliner to spend a lazy hour in the sun with the newspaper someone had left for them on a table in the living-room.

On the second page of the newspaper, dated two days after their marriage, she found something which made her sit up abruptly. It was a photograph of Jason and herself leaving the church, and she was surprised to see that her smile had a genuine appearance about it. Jason, too, was smiling faintly, and his appearance was a little less austere at that moment.

Melanie's glance rested on the pearl necklace about her neck, and she recalled her anger when his self-satisfied glance had rested on it briefly in the church. He had insisted that she should wear the necklace which had once belonged to his mother, and, although she had to admit that it suited her perfectly on that day, it had irked her to obey him, and she had returned the necklace into his safe keeping immediately after she had changed out of her wedding dress.

What had his mother been like? she wondered suddenly as she lowered the newspaper and stared at nothing in particular. There was so little she knew about Jason, she realised. She remembered him telling Granny Bridget that his parents had been killed in a small aircraft, but other than that there was really nothing she knew about him, except what the newspapers cared to print.

The air became chilly on the roof garden as time passed, and Melanie went inside, taking the newspaper with her to scrutinise at her leisure that evening while Jason was away at the office.

Was it work that kept Jason out so late, or was it Delia Cummings? she could not help wondering that night when she went to bed, tiredness snapping the tight rein she had had on her thoughts all afternoon.

Did it really matter where he was? Was it any concern of hers if he spent his time in the arms of another woman?

A peculiar tightness wound itself about her heart, and she turned on to her side, snapping off the light as she did so. Her thoughts dwelled on the past two weeks, and she recalled suddenly where she had heard the name 'Cummings' before. It had been in Jason's office that fateful day she had gone to see him to beg for leniency. He had told his secretary that, if Miss Cummings telephoned, she was to tell her that he would see her that evening.

What had been Delia's reaction, she wondered, when Jason had confronted her with the news that he intended marrying someone else? Had she been angry, Melanie wondered, or had she cleverly disguised her feelings? Was Jason with her now? Was he making love to her?

Dismissing her disturbing thoughts with a quality of fierceness she had not known she possessed, she turned over on to her other side and tried to sleep.

As they faced each other across the breakfast table, Melanie could not help thinking a little cynically that Jason looked remarkably fresh for a man who had worked until late the previous evening. He ate his breakfast in a relaxed, unhurried manner, and Melanie had the feeling that she did not exist until he raised his glance and captured hers relentlessly. His eyebrows rose sharply above those eternally mocking eyes, and she lowered her lashes swiftly to hide her confusion.

'I trust you slept well?'

The sarcasm in his tone stung her, but she managed to control the tremor in her voice as she murmured politely, 'Yes, thank you.'

'What are your plans for today?'

'I thought I'd pay a visit to Granny Bridget, and do a bit of shopping at the same time. The cupboards in the kitchen are practically empty, and what's left in the refrigerator has gone stale.'

'I seldom had a meal here at home, but buy whatever you think necessary, and have the accounts sent to me.' He removed a cheque book from his pocket and wrote out a cheque. 'That's for your own personal use.'

Melanie stared at the cheque he had pushed towards her across the table, and her breath locked in her throat momentarily as she stared at the amount. It was more than three months' salary put together, and the thought of accepting money from Jason, over and above that which her father had owed him, left a nasty taste in her mouth.

'Jason, I don't want——'

'What you do or don't want is of no concern. It's what I want that counts,' he interrupted coldly, draining his cup of coffee and ignoring the cheque she held out to him. 'I'll see you this evening.'

He was gone before she could prevent him and she jumped as he slammed the outer door behind him with unnecessary violence.

Left alone at the breakfast table with the cheque still clutched in her hand, she wondered what she should do. She did not want Jason's money; she would be too ashamed to use it. There was only one thing she could do, she decided eventually, and that was to tear up the cheque and say nothing about it to Jason. She took the cheque between her fingers, hesitated briefly, then ripped it to shreds with a determined yet satisfied look on her face before dropping the pieces into the wastepaper bin. Jason would never know, and she still had enough money of her own to last her several months if she did her personal shopping with care.

Granny Bridget was sitting in the living-room with a

rug across her legs when Melanie arrived at Greystone Manor later that morning, and her eyes lit up with pleasure at the sight of the slender, graceful figure of the young woman approaching her.

'Melanie child, it's good to see you,' she smiled as her hands were gripped firmly in Melanie's. 'I missed you.'

'I missed you too, Gran,' Melanie admitted, leaning forward to kiss the thin cheek before she examined her grandmother more closely. Granny Bridget's frailty had increased alarmingly, and there was concern in Melanie's eyes as she asked, 'Have you been well this past week?'

'I've been perfectly well, my dear,' her grandmother brushed aside her question with her usual impatience as she gestured towards the chair close to hers. 'Sit down and tell me about Jason and yourself. Are you happy?'

'Yes, Gran,' she lied, avoiding those shrewd blue eyes as she drew the chair closer and sat down.

'The mountain air has certainly done something for you, or is Jason the reason for the sparkle returning to your eyes, and that healthy flush on your cheeks?'

'Perhaps a little bit of both,' Melanie replied, hating herself for having to pretend to her grandmother as she skilfully steered the conversation in a different direction without drawing attention to the fact that she was reluctant to discuss her life with Jason.

They chatted for some time, but Melanie was surprised to discover that Granny Bridget was beginning to live very much in the past. She talked, at considerable length, of her son and others who had passed on before her, and Melanie was more than a little frightened when she became aware of the longing in Granny Bridget's voice, almost as if she wished the time would come for her to join her loved ones in the world beyond death.

'How is Granny Bridget's health?' Melanie demanded of Sister Wilson when she cornered her on her way out.

'She's as well as can be expected, my dear.'

'Don't be evasive,' Melanie accused as she searched the expressionless face of the uniformed Sister who had become almost a part of the family during the past months. 'I want the truth ... please!'

Sister Wilson looked away. 'Perhaps you should speak to the doctor. He——'

'I'm asking *you*!' Melanie insisted, fear clutching at her heart.

'Melanie, my dear ...' Sister Wilson took one look at the stubborn determination on the face of the young woman before her, and capitulated with a sigh of acceptance. 'Her health is deteriorating rapidly.'

'How rapidly?'

'That's difficult to say.' The older woman seemed to fidget uncomfortably beneath Melanie's direct gaze. 'Ever since your father's death she's failed to respond to treatment as well as she used to.'

Melanie stared at her incredulously. 'You mean she's losing the will to live?'

'It seems so, yes.'

'I see.'

With her suspicions confirmed that Granny Bridget no longer had the desire to live, Melanie felt herself weighed down by a helplessness that brought her to the verge of tears. Life without her grandmother was unthinkable, but it was inevitable, and there was nothing she could do to halt the process of nature.

'I'm sorry, Melanie.'

She blinked away the glimmer of tears in her eyes and smiled a little wanly. 'I asked for the truth, Sister Wilson, and I'm grateful to you for being so honest with me.'

Melanie walked blindly from the house and down the

driveway towards the bus stop a block away. Her mind was so busy assimilating the details of her conversation with Sister Wilson that she stared without recognition at the Chev that drew up beside her, and the chestnut-haired young man who leaned across from the driver's seat to open the door nearest to her.

'Melanie!'

The sound of her name brought her to her senses, and recognition sharpened her glance. 'Adrian! What are you doing here?'

'I've been waiting for you.'

'How did you know I would be here this morning?' she asked curiously, ignoring the silent invitation of the door he held open for her.

'I telephoned last night to find out if anyone had heard from you, and Sister Wilson told me you were expected this morning,' Adrian explained, his smile charming and persuasive. 'Get in, and I'll drive you to wherever you want to be.'

Knowing how he felt about her made her hesitate. 'It's kind of you, Adrian, but——'

'I must talk to you, Melanie,' he interrupted urgently. 'Please?'

His pleading glance swayed her decision. 'Would I be taking you out of your way if I asked you to drive me to the city?'

'I'm going that way myself,' he smiled. 'Get in.'

Melanie obeyed him silently and Adrian pulled way from the curb with unnecessary speed. She glanced at his silent, boyish profile, and the seriousness of his expression aroused her curiosity.

'You said you wanted to talk to me,' she prompted him gently.

'Are you happy, Melanie?' he asked, and she looked away hastily to hide the wariness in her eyes.

'Yes, of course.'

'Are you sure?'

'Jason hasn't ill-treated me in any way, if that's what you were hoping for,' she assured him a little too sharply.

'Calm down, Melanie,' he said quietly, applying the brake and parking the car in a parking area beside a children's play park.

Alarm mingled with curiosity. 'Why are we stopping?'

'I want to talk to you,' he replied, switching off the ignition and turning to face her.

'Surely you can drive and talk at the same time?'

'Melanie ...' He leaned towards her, his hazel eyes intent upon her face. 'I know about the loan your father took from Jason Kerr.'

Her expression became guarded as a tremor of shock rippled through her. 'Do you?'

'I also know about Greystone Manor being offered as security,' Adrian continued, ignoring the signs that should have told him that he had gone too far.

'I don't know where you got all this information from, but——'

'Did Jason Kerr force you into this marriage?'

He had guessed the truth so accurately that she snapped defensively, 'Don't be absurd!'

'Look at me!'

Taking her chin in his hand, he forced her to meet his eyes, and Melanie resorted to anger as her only defence. 'You have no right to question me like this, Adrian.'

'I happen to love you,' he stated calmly, 'and loving you gives me the right to be concerned about you.'

'There's no need for you to concern yourself,' she said abruptly, brushing his hand aside.

'Melanie——'

'Who told you about the loan my father made?'

'I'm afraid I can't disclose my source of information,

but it's remarkable how much a tongue can be loosened after a few free drinks,' he replied unashamedly, and Melanie stared at him for a few moments in shocked, angry silence.

'I think you're despicable!' she said at last, and her voice was as cold as she felt at that moment. 'You had no right to pry into something which didn't concern you, and as for the loan my father made, it was, and still is, a private matter between my husband and myself.'

My husband. It was the first time she had referred to Jason in that capacity, but she was too angry to be more than vaguely aware of it as she saw a flush of embarrassment stain Adrian's cheeks.

'What I did, I did out of concern for you.'

'That's still no excuse for your behaviour,' she stated firmly, wrenching open the door and stepping out of the car.

'Where are you going?' Adrian demanded anxiously.

'I'll catch a bus round the next corner,' she flung at him as she walked away.

'Don't be ridiculous!'

'Goodbye, Adrian,' she said with a finality that finally penetrated through to him and halted him in the process of following her.

Realising that she could not remain in Adrian's company under the circumstances, she walked on without looking back and was fortunate enough to reach the bus stop just as a bus approached. She paid for her ticket and sat down staring blindly out of the window until her anger had subsided sufficiently for her to think clearly. She should not have lost her temper with Adrian, she realised ruefully. It would, perhaps, have been more convincing to laugh off Adrian's remarks, but it was too late now to alter the situation, and she could only hope that he would keep his findings to himself.

Restless and worried about her grandmother, she

sought refuge on the roof garden after dinner that evening. The lights of the city lay spread out before her, neon signs flickered invitingly, and the distant hum of traffic indicated the seemingly endless activity of those who went in search of entertainment. It was like standing in the middle of a restless beehive, and she hated it more and more as she thought of the peace and tranquillity she had always enjoyed at Greystone Manor.

The sound of a step behind her made her turn, and her pulse quickened ridiculously as Jason leaned against the wall beside her and finished his cigarette in silence. His white shirt, unbuttoned to the waist, accentuated his tanned fitness in the light that shone out from the living-room, and Melanie's senses were instantly alert to the onslaught of his masculinity. The brooding intensity of his steel-grey eyes as he stood observing her succeeded in unnerving her, and she said the first thing that came into her head to relieve the tension that was beginning to spiral through her.

'Do you enjoy living way up here in this concrete jungle?'

'It's convenient.'

'It's claustrophobic,' she corrected abruptly, turning from him to avoid the strange magnetism he seemed to exude.

'Are you missing Greystone Manor already?'

A lump rose unbidden to her throat and, ignoring his question, she said tritely, 'I saw my grandmother this morning.'

'How is she?'

'Her health isn't improving at all.'

'What did you expect for someone her age?'

'I don't know, but I certainly didn't think she would give up without a fight.' She swallowed with difficulty and clenched her fists on the wall. 'I wish there was something I could do.'

'You can't prevent the will of God, Melanie.'

She bit her lip, fighting back the tears, but she could not hide the tremor in her voice as she whispered, 'I know ... and it makes me feel so helpless.'

He turned her to face him, and his touch was warm and pleasing against her shoulders. 'If you could, you would move heaven and earth for those you love, wouldn't you?'

Melanie was too choked to reply, and all at once too aware of his nearness, and the clean male scent of him, to think of anything else. The breeze lifted her hair, blowing it across her face like a silvery veil, and Jason raised his hand to remove it, his fingers lingering for a moment in the silky strands before they slid caressingly across her cheek and her throat.

'I have a feeling that, when you love, you will love completely and absolutely,' he continued, the deep vibrancy of his voice having an odd effect on her nerves as he added, 'There'll be no half measures attached to the giving of yourself.'

Something warned her that she was being carefully and deliberately seduced, but her limbs refused to obey the urgent commands of her brain. She stood perfectly still beneath his hands, her pulse racing, and her senses responding deliciously to his touch. 'Run!' her brain urged again, but the warning came too late. There was no escape from the arms that held her and the mouth which had descended upon hers with a sensuality that drew an instant response from her. But, more than anything, she was trapped by the unexpected storm of her own clamouring emotions.

Jason's hands were warm against her skin beneath her sweater, and she trembled at the sensations they aroused. She was vaguely aware of her bra being loosened, but she no longer cared. Her arms went up to circle his neck, and a shudder of ecstasy shook through her when she felt the touch of his hands against her breasts.

'You've been a tantalising and elusive little witch,' he laughed triumphantly against her throat. 'Your surrender will be adequate compensation for the loss of my freedom.'

Sanity returned with an acute sense of shame at the thought of how easily she had succumbed and, with her emotions taking a swift downward plunge, she caught him off guard and broke free with an agile twist of her slender body.

'*Your freedom?*' she gasped incredulously, resentment fanning her anger as she stared up into his arrogant face. 'What about the loss of *my* freedom?'

'I valued my freedom very much, but let's not quibble about it,' he laughed, reaching for her, but she stepped back smartly and placed a deck chair between them.

'I gave up my freedom for a worthy cause, which is something you can't claim to have done,' she cried in a choked voice, trembling uncontrollably, and horrifyingly close to tears. 'If I could wish for anything, I would wish that I'd never set eyes on you. You're arrogant, self-opinionated, and I *hate* you!'

With one lithe movement the chair was swept aside, and she was taken roughly by the shoulders and shaken until she felt certain her neck would snap, then he dragged her against him, his strong fingers gripping her face painfully as he forced her to look up into his furious eyes.

'You may think you hate me,' he accused in a harsh voice, 'but I happen to know that you're not as insensitive to me as you would like me to believe.'

'Let me go! You're hurting me!' she gasped as tears gathered in her eyes.

'I'll let you go when I've had my say, and not before,' he rasped, slackening his hold, but not releasing her. 'I could have you now, if I wanted to, and I'm willing to bet that you wouldn't offer much resistance either, but the moment has passed, and so has the inclination. Think it over, Melanie, and think about this as well.'

He bent over her, his muscular thighs hard against her own as he curved her body into his, and she was powerless to resist when his mouth fastened on to hers with a ruthlessness which was a punishment as well as a revelation. There was a great deal of truth in his statement, for she could not fight against her treacherous emotions any more than she could fight against his superior strength, and she relinquished the struggle, allowing herself to be swept along on a tide of sensations until she hovered on the brink of desire.

Her surrender would have meant an uncontested victory for Jason, but she was unexpectedly freed, and shivering without the warmth of his arms about her. It had come as something of a surprise, and more so his cool, detached appearance while her emotions were in such a frantic turmoil.

'You'd better go inside.'

His voice was clipped and cold, and Melanie stared at him blankly for a moment, her trembling lips still warm and tingling from his kisses. Suddenly nothing made sense any more, and she turned and fled, engulfed in a wave of shame, and choking on unshed tears when she finally closed her bedroom door behind her and leaned against it weakly.

'What's happening to me?' she wondered, humiliated and confused by what had occurred. 'For a moment out there I actually wanted him to make love to me. I wanted it so badly I wouldn't have cared what he thought of me afterwards.'

Alarmed at the nature of her thoughts, she tried to brush them aside, but they persisted relentlessly until the awful truth was made agonisingly clear to her.

'I can't be in love with him!' she whispered anxiously to herself as she walked unsteadily across to the bed and sat down heavily. 'I can't be in love with a man as ruthless and hard as Jason; a man who has never hidden the fact that he's sought feminine company in the past merely to satisfy his sexual desires. I can't possibly love a man like *that*!'

She pressed her fingers against her throbbing temples and closed her eyes in an effort to shut out the unbearable facts, but there was no escape from the dreadful realisation of what had happened to her. She had given her love to a man who had no need of it. He wanted her body, and that was all! When he was tired of her, he would end their marriage and seek someone else. It was an agonisingly painful thought, but she had to face facts. It was no use dreaming dreams of an idyllic future when there was no possibility of those dreams coming true. Above all else, she had to be realistic.

She heard Jason moving about in his room, opening and closing cupboards, and a few minutes later the outer door slammed shut. He was on his way to Delia Cummings, no doubt, to seek solace in her waiting arms.

Melanie winced at the thought and tried to shrug it off as she prepared herself for bed, but the hurt persisted and her pillow was damp with tears when she eventually fell asleep.

CHAPTER SIX

THE doorbell chimed just before ten the following morning, and Melanie found a lean young man with unruly dark hair and smiling brown eyes standing on the doorstep.

'Mrs Kerr?'

It was the first time anyone had addressed her as such, and she couldn't quite make up her mind how she felt about it at that moment as she murmured, 'Yes?'

'I'm Barnaby Finch,' he smiled, extending his hand and clasping Melanie's firmly. 'I'm liaison officer and general odd-job man for Mr Kerr,' he explained.

'I see.'

'I don't think you do, ma'am,' he grinned as she stood aside for him to enter, 'and right this minute you're most probably wondering what the heck I'm doing here.'

His perceptiveness amused her and she laughed softly as she led the way into the living-room. 'You're quite right, Mr Finch, I *am* curious to know why my husband's liaison officer should pay me a visit.'

'First of all, ma'am, the name is Barnaby. No one calls me anything else. And secondly, the boss told me to come round this morning to present myself to you.' His expression sobered as he sat down opposite her. 'I'm told that your grandmother is ill, ma'am, and until the boss has time to find a suitable car for you, I'm at your service.'

Bewildered by this disclosure, she said a little sharply, 'That's very thoughtful of my husband, and I

99

appreciate your offer, but I'm really quite capable of taking a bus.'

'That may be so, ma'am, but I'm under orders to drive you wherever you want to go.' He placed a printed card on the small table in front of her. 'You'll find me at that telephone number any time during the day.'

'Mr Finch ... Barnaby,' she corrected herself hastily when he grimaced comically. 'I hate the idea of being a nuisance to anyone.'

Barnaby's grin broadened, and he looked a little embarrassed as he pushed his bony fingers through his unruly crop of hair. 'To be quite honest, ma'am, I hated the idea myself, but now that I've met you, I'm looking forward to being your personal chauffeur for a time.'

Amusement lifted the corners of her mouth, and banished the shadows which lurked in her eyes. 'It's kind of you to say so, Barnaby, and I find your honesty praiseworthy.'

He shifted a little uncomfortably in his chair. 'Did you wish to go anywhere this morning, ma'am?'

'Well, I ...'

'To see your grandmother, perhaps?' he prompted eagerly as she hesitated.

'Yes, I was thinking of going out to Greystone Manor again this morning, but——'

'Then I'll drive you there,' Barnaby interrupted, jumping to his feet with an eagerness that made her follow suit involuntarily. 'If you'll get yourself ready, ma'am, I'll use the telephone in the study to let the boss know where I'll be.'

Melanie nodded absently and left him to do the necessary while she went through to her bedroom to grab her coat and handbag. Barnaby obviously knew his way around the penthouse, she thought as she checked her make-up and pulled a comb through her hair, and she could not help wondering what he, and the other members of Jason's staff, thought of their employer's unexpected marriage.

'Are you comfortable, ma'am?' Barnaby enquired as he slid behind the wheel of the Mercedes, and Melanie winced, not for the first time, at the word 'ma'am'.

'I'm quite comfortable, thank you ... and Barnaby,' she turned slightly in her seat to face him as he steered the car into the stream of traffic, 'if we're going to see quite a lot of each other in future, do you think you could dispense with the "ma'am" and just call me Melanie?'

'The boss doesn't encourage familiarity, ma'am.'

That was not surprising, she thought to herself, and she could not imagine anyone getting close enough to Jason to know the real man beneath that hard exterior.

'Then I shall have to retaliate by calling you "Mr Finch" in future.'

Barnaby grimaced. 'I don't think I could stand that.'

'What about making it Melanie, then, when we're alone?'

'You're the prettiest blackmailer I've ever met ... Melanie,' he added laughingly, glancing at her briefly before concentrating on the road once more. 'I just hope I remember to call you "ma'am" when the boss is around, or I shall find myself minus a job!'

The drive out to Greystone Manor seemed shorter than usual in Barnaby's company. Once the ice was broken they had chatted like old friends, and Melanie had found him entertaining in a comical but serious way.

'What time shall I call for you again?' he wanted to know as he assisted her gallantly from the car.

'I think I'll stay and have lunch with my grandmother today, so what about three this afternoon?'

'Fine,' he smiled, raising his hand in a brief salute as he walked round to the driver's side. 'See you later, Melanie.'

She stared after the Mercedes as it disappeared down the drive and stood a moment longer to drink in the sun-drenched beauty of the garden with its trees and shrubs and spacious lawns. This was her very own paradise; a paradise she would lose one day because of her father's recklessness, and Jason was to be the one who would take it from her. There was despair in her glance as it roamed the gardens and the old stone house, but she pulled herself together quickly when she saw the lace curtain at the living-room window being drawn agitatedly aside. Granny Bridget was becoming impatient.

'Who was that young man, Melanie?' her grandmother demanded almost before she had time to greet her properly.

'He's Jason's liaison officer, Barnaby Finch,' Melanie explained, drawing a pouffe closer and seating herself at her grandmother's feet. 'Jason has asked him to act as my chauffeur for a while until I have a car of my own.'

'How very kind of Jason!'

'I don't think I should allow him to be so generous, though.'

'Why ever not?'

Melanie avoided Granny Bridget's curious glance and stared out of the window. 'I don't like the idea of Jason spending money on me.'

'But he's your husband!' the old woman stated incredulously. 'It's only natural that he would want to buy you gifts.'

'A car is rather an expensive gift,' Melanie laughed shakily.

'He can afford it.'

'Oh, Gran!' she groaned, the intended rebuke dying

on her lips at the look of innocence on her grand-mother's face.

'I'm worried about you, my child. You were so evasive yesterday, and so quick to change the subject.' Those faded blue eyes searched Melanie's. 'You haven't, by any chance, discovered that you've made a mistake?'

Melanie shook her head and looked away. 'Of course not, Gran.'

'Look at me, Melanie,' she instructed, and Melanie obeyed reluctantly. 'Do you love Jason?'

Her body tensed and the muscles in her throat ached as she said stiffly, 'Yes.'

'Don't lie to me, Melanie. I want the truth.'

'I'm *not* lying. I——' The tension snapped inside her, and she buried her face in her grandmother's lap as the hot tears filled her eyes and cascaded down her pale cheeks. 'Granny Bridget, I think I love him so much that I feel quite sick inside!'

It was useless trying to pretend to herself that nothing had happened. The discovery of her love for Jason was something she could not ignore. It had taken possession of her so entirely that she knew, without doubt, that she would never quite be the same again.

'I know, child,' Granny Bridget soothed her, stroking Melanie's silky hair much in the same way as she had done when Melanie had been a child. 'I loved your grandfather like that, and sometimes the slightest gesture of impatience used to wound me most deeply.' Her hand ceased its caressing movements. 'Have you had a tiff with Jason?'

'Yes ... and no,' Melanie sighed as she sat up and searched for a handkerchief in her handbag.

'My poor Melanie,' Granny Bridget smiled tenderly while Melanie dried her eyes and blew her nose. 'Everything always happens for the best, and these little arguments often help to clear the air.'

Melanie pulled herself together with an effort. 'It

wasn't my intention to come here and cry on your shoulder, Gran.'

'I know,' the old woman patted her arm and glanced over Melanie's shoulder. 'Ah, Sister Wilson, you've brought the tea. Melanie and I can both do with a cup.'

The subject was never mentioned again, and Melanie tried to shake off her depression for her grandmother's sake. As the day progressed, however, she found it easier to shift her own problems into the background when she noticed how easily her grandmother tired. On several occasions during the morning she had dropped off to sleep in her chair, only to awaken a few minutes later to continue the conversation as if nothing had happened. It disturbed Melanie to see her like this, but Sister Wilson seemed to take it all in her stride.

Barnaby arrived punctually at three that afternoon, and Melanie let him in. 'My grandmother is resting,' she explained as she led the way, 'but I've had a tray of tea brought through to the living-room.'

'Hm ... old, but nice,' he remarked as he looked about him with interest.

'Greystone Manor *is* rather old, and it needs renovating badly, but ...' She hesitated, realising that she was pursuing a hopeless subject, and asked, 'Do you take milk and sugar?'

'Milk and two spoons of sugar, please,' Barnaby replied with an infectious grin. 'I have a sweet tooth.'

'So have I,' she admitted, handing him his tea.

'That's very realistic,' Barnaby remarked at length, gesturing towards the painting above the fireplace. It was of a hunter standing behind a bush, his rifle lowered as he admired the herd of springbok grazing in the veld. 'Is it an original?'

'My grandfather used to do a little painting in his spare time, I believe,' she explained. 'He went on several safaris in his youth, but he hated having to use his gun. He painted that from memory, and it's really quite appropriate.'

'The boss did a bit of hunting as well some years ago.'

Melanie nodded. 'I've seen the mounted head of the lion he shot adorning the lounge of his chalet, and it's quite horrifying.'

'Oh, but he didn't shoot that lion, Melanie,' Barnaby corrected hastily. 'He killed it with his hunting knife. Didn't he tell you?'

Bewildered, she said: 'I know about the lion hunt, but I assumed he'd shot it.'

'No,' Barnaby shook his head adamantly. 'One of the team members was trigger-happy and shot too soon, and the lion was merely wounded. It was one heck of a to-do which ended with the boss and the farmer's son going into the bush after it.' He pushed a bony hand through his hair, looking a little uncertain as to whether he should continue, then, making up his mind, he added, 'To cut a long story short, they walked right into the enraged animal's hiding place, and it attacked the farmer's son. The boss's rifle jammed at the crucial moment, and he straddled the beast, killing it with his hunting knife.'

Melanie understood now why Jason had not wanted to discuss the subject, and her heart swelled with pride. 'He saved a man's life.'

'And has the scars to prove it,' Barnaby added quietly.

'Scars?'

'You must have seen the scars on the inside of his left arm where the lion's teeth had ripped open the flesh during the struggle?'

'Oh! ... Oh, yes,' she muttered, covering up her ignorance as best she could. 'Is that why he had the lion's head mounted?'

'No,' Barnaby grinned mischievously. 'It was a gift

from the farmer, and one which the boss couldn't refuse.' His expression sobered instantly. 'Very few people
know of this incident, Melanie.'

'And my husband doesn't like discussing it either,'
she summed up the situation swiftly.

'No.'

'I can understand that,' she spoke her thoughts out
loud. 'But it was an extremely courageous and wonderful thing to do. Not many people would have risked
their lives to save someone else's.'

Barnaby fingered his chin. 'I think it embarrasses him
to talk about it.'

Why should it embarrass him? she wondered silently.
Was he perhaps afraid that people might suspect he was
human after all? There were so many things she did not
know about the man she had married, Melanie realised
yet again. At first she had not cared, but now, loving
him as she did, she was filled with an insatiable curiosity.

'How long have you been working for my husband?'
she questioned Barnaby.

'Six years or so.'

'You must know him quite well, then?'

Barnaby nodded thoughtfully. 'I think so, yes.'

'I suppose it came as a surprise to learn of our marriage,' she remarked after a slight hesitation, guiding
the conversation in the direction of the subject which
perturbed her most.

'I'll say it did!' Barnaby laughed.

'Most especially, I suppose, because of my husband's
friendship with Delia Cummings?'

Barnaby's bony face stiffened in the chair opposite
her. 'You know about her?'

'Yes.'

'I don't suppose it was as serious as we all thought,'
he said evasively, glancing at his wristwatch.

'What's she like, Barnaby?' she continued to question him, eager to know more about the woman who was so certain of her hold over Jason.

'She's very beautiful.'

'Is that all?' Melanie laughed disappointedly.

Barnaby looked away. 'I must get back to the office, Melanie, much as I enjoy chatting to you.'

Melanie sighed inwardly as Barnaby got to his feet. She would get nothing more from Barnaby, and her curiosity would have to remain unsatisfied.

'You're very loyal, Barnaby,' she said quietly, throwing her coat over her arm and smiling up at him. 'I hope some of that loyalty extends my way too?'

To her amazement he flushed a dull red before going absolutely white. 'Whatever we've discussed, Melanie, will remain only between us, but I have a confession to make.'

Melanie felt herself grow tense and said a little unsteadily, 'You make it sound terribly serious.'

'It is serious.' He avoided her eyes and stared down at the carpet. 'I know about the money your father borrowed from the boss.'

'Is that all?' she demanded quietly, keeping a rigid control on the wild thoughts racing through her mind.

'No,' he shook his head, and there was a silent plea in the eyes that met hers now. 'I met a close friend of yours one evening, and I'm afraid I told him about it.'

Melanie went cold. 'I presume you're referring to Adrian Louw?'

'That's right.' His expression was grim. 'I had no intention of giving him this information, but . . .'

'It all sort of came out after a couple of drinks,' she finished for him dryly as she recalled her conversation with Adrian the previous day.

Barnaby stared at her quizzically. 'How did you know . . . about the drinks, I mean?'

'Never mind,' she said, forcing a smile to her lips. 'Thank you for telling me, and don't give the matter another thought.'

Barnaby was contrite, but she managed to make him snap out of it by the time they arrived in the city, and he was his usual smiling self when he eventually left her on the doorstep of the penthouse.

The telephone was ringing in the study when she entered and, dropping her coat over the back of a chair, she went through to answer it.

'Melanie, I've been trying to reach you all day,' Adrian's voice came over the line.

'I've been out at Greystone Manor most of the day,' she replied, and her voice was cool with the effort to suppress her anger. 'What did you want, Adrian?'

'I wanted to apologise for some of the things I said yesterday, and I was hoping you would have tea with me one afternoon next week.'

Melanie's fingers tightened on the receiver. 'As a matter of fact, there is something I would like to discuss with you, so it would suit me fine.'

'Shall we say next week Tuesday at the Carlton, then, at about three?' he suggested, sounding a little surprised that he had had no difficulty in persuading her.

'I'll be there.'

'Good!' he said happily. 'See you then, my dear.'

She replaced the receiver and stood for a moment contemplating her decision. It was perhaps not wise of her to have accepted his invitation, but she was determined to tell him exactly what she thought of him and, to do that, she had to meet him face to face.

During the next few days, as Barnaby drove her to and from Greystone manor, she discovered that, contrary to what she had suspected, Jason had been spending many hours at the office working on a tender for the new steel plant which was to be erected on the East Rand. It was comforting to know that Delia Cummings was not the cause of the irregular hours he had kept, but it did nothing to alleviate the tense situation which had developed between Jason and herself. He remained cool and polite whenever they were together, making it impossible for Melanie to get close to him, and she was beginning to despair that she would ever be able to reach him.

It was at the end of that week, at a banquet for business men and their wives which was held at the home of one of Jason's associates, that Melanie met Delia Cummings for the first time, and it was not difficult to see why Jason had been so captivated.

Tall, dark, and incredibly slender, she was the most beautiful woman Melanie had ever seen, and her 'Jason darling!' rang out only too clearly above the noise as she made her way towards them. The shimmering black off-the-shoulder evening gown suited her colouring, and clung to her figure in a way that made many of the women glance at her enviously. But Melanie was more interested in her heavily lashed liquid-brown eyes beneath perfectly arched brows, and the sensuously curved red mouth which was pouting slightly as she slipped her arm possessively through Jason's.

'How good it is to see you again,' she purred up at him, but those beautiful eyes had lost a little of their warmth when they met Melanie's. 'Do introduce me to your wife, darling.'

No one would have guessed that they had so much as spoken to each other before, and Melanie could not help but admire Delia for her acting ability while Jason introduced them formally. He made no effort either to shake off those slender, manicured hands clutching at his arm, and Melanie had the horrible feeling that several pairs of eyes were observing them with interest and a great deal of curious speculation.

'My dear, I've been dying to meet you, and we must get together some time for a chat. Jason and I are, after all, such *old* friends. Aren't we, darling?' Delia demanded, the warmth in her voice as she gazed up at him suggesting a certain intimacy that sent a stab of unaccustomed jealousy tearing through Melanie.

'You're slipping, Delia,' Jason acused lightly. 'There was a time when you would never have used the word "old" when referring to yourself.'

'You're a brute, darling, and I don't know why I take these little jibes from you,' Delia retorted calmly as she released his arm. 'Be a dear and fetch me a drink.'

Jason's eyes sought Melanie's. 'I won't be a moment.'

She nodded stiffly, suppressing the desire to follow his tall figure across the room as she experienced a rush of panic at the thought of being alone with this woman who no longer made any pretence of friendliness.

'I gather you never told Jason of our telephone conversation?'

'No.'

'That was very wise of you, my dear,' Delia smiled with satisfaction, a glimmer of triumph in her cold eyes. 'Men never like to think that their actions are predictable to women.'

'You still seem very sure that he'll come running back to you.'

'There's no doubt about it, darling. I know him too well to be mistaken about that,' Delia stated with a confidence that filled Melanie with cold despair. 'You haven't the qualities to hold a man like Jason,' she continued, her glance contemptuous as she took in Melanie's small slenderness in the flowing cream-coloured silk. 'Before very long he'll tire of your appealing, childlike innocence, and he'll realise that only a woman like myself could satisfy him completely.'

Melanie clenched her hand at her side as she felt the rising urge to slap that smug look off Delia Cummings' beautiful face. This woman was calculatingly clever, and for the moment she had the upper hand, leaving Melanie defenceless and painfully aware of it.

Jason made his way towards them through the crowd, and Melanie almost cried with relief as she spotted him, but she controlled herself hastily as he reached their side.

'Your drink, Delia.'

'Darling, you're an angel!'

Their hands touched as Delia took the glass from him, but Melanie felt certain that it was a deliberate action on Delia's part to drive home the validity of her statements, although Jason appeared not to notice anything out of the ordinary as he glanced across the room with interest.

'If you'll excuse us, Delia, I'd like to have a word with McAlister.'

Delia accepted this gracefully, and Melanie felt his hand beneath her elbow as he guided her across the room towards the elderly gentleman who stood nursing his drink beside the potted fern in the corner. The introductions were made, and Melanie knew at once that this short, rather stout man was the one whose decision would determine whether Jason gained the contract for the new steel plant or not.

'I can see now why Jason was in such an infernal hurry to give up his bachelor days,' he remarked, his admiring glance making the colour return to her pale cheeks. 'If I were thirty years younger he might have had severe competition.'

'It's kind of you to say so, Mr McAlister,' she smiled, disengaging her hand from his as she became aware of Jason's mocking glance.

'Mac, can we talk business?'

'Certainly, my dear chap,' McAlister said agreeably, and Melanie decided tactfully that it was time for her to melt away into the distance.

'I think I'll take a stroll out on to the terrace,' she excused herself, and walked away quickly towards the french windows.

Drawing her wrap closer about her shoulders, she stepped out on to the terrace and shivered as she felt the coldness of the night air wafting against her body. There was hardly a moon in the sky, and the darkness seemed to envelop her as she strolled further along the terrace to where the honeysuckle ranked profusely on a trellis which formed an adequate partition. She slipped behind it quickly, relishing the seclusion it offered from the noise inside, and from Delia Cummings who was in the midst of it, making a determined effort, no doubt, to make Jason aware of what he had relinquished by marrying someone else.

It had been a humiliating experience meeting Delia, but she supposed it had had to happen some time. Now she at least knew exactly what she was up against, and something told her that Delia would not give up easily.

Melanie sighed, brushing aside the unpleasant thoughts which disturbed her so much, and making an effort to regain the composure she had lost so completely in Delia's presence. There was one thing which was very clear to her, however. Jason must never guess how she felt about him!

Lost in her thoughts, she had no idea how long she remained there on the terrace, but she was certain that almost half an hour had passed when the sound of a woman's clear voice brought her sharply back to the present.

'Delia Cummings looks younger every time I see her. I wonder how she manages it.'

'And that figure!' her female companion exclaimed.

'Yes, but then she seldom does more than nibble at her food.'

'I suppose that if you're a model, and you want to stay at the top of your profession, you just have to be careful what you eat.'

Melanie was in a quandary whether to show herself, or not, when the first woman said something which made her shrink deeper into the shadows.

'I wonder how it must feel to come face to face with your husband's mistress?'

Melanie held her breath as the woman's companion stressed, '*Ex*-mistress.'

'I wonder ...' mused the first woman. 'Things have been pretty hot between them during the past two years, and I can't see Delia giving up without a fight.'

Melanie wished fervently that she had shown herself before the conversation had gone this far, but there was nothing she could do at that moment except remain where she was if she did not want to humiliate herself further.

'Jason's wife is very pretty,' the conversation between the two women continued.

'Yes, but she's not much of a match for Delia,' the lady with the clear, precise voice argued. 'Delia has plenty of experience to draw on and, quite frankly, I wouldn't want to be in Melanie Kerr's shoes right now.'

'Do you think Delia has plans to break up their marriage?'

'I don't just think it, I *know* it. Didn't you see the clever way she got Jason away from old McAlister and lured him into the garden a few minutes ago?'

Melanie felt as though someone had delivered a fatal blow to the most vulnerable spot in her midriff, and she clutched at the wall behind her as her legs began to shake beneath her.

'No, I didn't,' the conversation went on.

'Well, you can be sure it wasn't just for a friendly chat they sought the seclusion of this enormous garden. I only hope that his wife never saw them leave.'

They moved away from Melanie's hiding place, but even so, she was no longer listening to what they were saying. Jason was somewhere in this garden with Delia, was all she could think of, and she groaned inwardly at the visions that sprang to mind. Delia had wasted little time in her pursuit of Jason, and he had apparently offered little resistance to the prospect of a few amorous moments in the secluded garden with the woman who had once been his mistress ... and who, perhaps, would continue to be his mistress if he received enough encouragement.

The thought was tearing Melanie apart, and she ran from the shadows of the honeysuckle, dry-eyed and pale, only to collide seconds later with a stocky figure emerging from the shadows further along the terrace.

'Oh!' she gasped as hands steadied her, and then she saw who it was. 'I'm terribly sorry, Mr McAlister, I didn't see you in the darkness.'

'I came out for a breath of fresh air. That's what I hate about these parties, my dear, it's always so stuffy indoors,' he confided in her. 'I don't suppose you would consider keeping an old man company, would you?'

'I wouldn't mind at all,' she assured him, grateful suddenly that she would not be alone while Jason ... !

She pulled herself up smartly, making a violent effort to control her thoughts as she joined Mr McAlister on a wooden bench nearby.

'You know, that husband of yours drives a very hard bargain,' he said eventually, the aroma of his cigar floating about her.

'Does he?' she asked stiffly, reluctant to speak of the one person who had it in his power to hurt her more than anyone else on earth.

'Do you know about the new steel plant we want to

erect on the East Rand?' Mr McAlister questioned her.

'I've heard of it, yes.'

'Steel Incorporated has been taking a look at tenders from engineering firms all over the country, and we've eliminated all but two companies; Cyma, which is your husband's, and Reef Engineering. It's a very difficult decision to make.'

Melanie had no idea why he should be discussing this subject with her, but it was at least helping her to shake off the misery she felt.

'Which are the most important factors when it comes to a selection such as this?' she questioned him a little absently.

'Well, there are the plans put forward by the firms, and the quality of their workmanship.'

'Does the cost of such a scheme have anything to do with your decision?'

'Very much indeed, and that's what makes it so difficult. I like what Jason is offering us, for instance, but his price is a little high.' He puffed agitatedly at his cigar for a few seconds, then glanced at her speculatively through a haze of smoke. 'What would you do if you were in my position?'

'I'm afraid I don't know enough about my husband's business to comment on that, and I wouldn't want to influence you one way or the other,' she replied, a little startled that he should ask for her meagre opinion.

Mr McAlister removed his cigar from his mouth and nodded his grey head thoughtfully. 'A very sensible answer, and one which has put you way up in my estimation, but off the record, what would you do?' He touched her arm as she hesitated and said: 'Go ahead. Don't be afraid to give your opinion.'

Reassured, she said: 'Speaking from personal experience only, when I've wanted anything of value I've always ended up paying more for it, but I've never regretted it afterwards.'

Mr McAlister was silent for several alarming seconds, his cigar forgotten between his fingers, then he turned to her and smiled. 'You know, my dear, you've certainly given me something to think about.'

Melanie was not quite sure what to make of that remark, but Mr McAlister gave her no opportunity to ponder over it for too long. He chatted amicably for a while longer, then took her inside with him to introduce her to his wife, a small, pleasant-looking woman whom Melanie liked instantly. They both displayed a great deal of tact, Melanie thought afterwards, by not remarking on Jason's noticeable absence and, when he calmly put in an appearance later, she felt mentally and physically strengthened to cope with the immediate situation.

The evening dragged on endlessly, and she was immeasurably relieved when Jason finally suggested that it was time to go. The McAlisters were leaving as well and, as they parted company on the way to their respective cars, Mr McAlister said:

'I'll see you at your office on Monday morning, Jason, then we can put the deal through.'

Melanie held her breath as Jason demanded calmly, 'Does this mean you've made up your mind to accept my tender, Mac?'

'It does,' McAlister assured him, 'and you can thank your lovely wife for that.'

The McAlisters' car sped down the driveway, and its occupants were quite unaware of the explosive situation which had developed as a result of that innocent, light-hearted remark. Melanie could feel Jason's eyes boring through her in the darkness. She tried to say something, but couldn't, and relinquished the effort eventually, deciding that it could wait until Jason had cooled off sufficiently.

CHAPTER SEVEN

THE atmosphere in the car had been tense, but Melanie shrank inwardly from the cold fury in Jason's pale grey eyes as he closed the penthouse door behind him with a decisive click and followed her through to the living-room.

'Would you kindly explain to me what McAlister meant by that parting shot of his?' His deep voice vibrated with anger, but she was almost relieved that the storm was about to erupt. Anything was preferable to his stony silence, she decided as he snapped, 'I'm waiting!'

She gathered the remnants of her courage about her and explained, as calmly as she could, what had occurred between Mr McAlister and herself. Jason heard her out in silence, but a cynical smile curved his lips.

'It seems that having a wife can be an asset after all.'

Stung by his remark, she said sarcastically, 'Does it hurt your pride to think that, inadvertently, I accomplished something in a short space of time which might have taken you longer?'

Jason went white about the mouth and for a moment she thought he would strike her, but he controlled himself with a visible effort and said cuttingly, 'When it comes to business, Melanie, I prefer doing things *my* way, and not from behind a woman's skirts.'

'I had no intention of influencing him, Jason, and Mr McAlister was well aware of that,' she told him quietly. 'He insisted on hearing my opinion and, for what it was worth, I gave it to him. If the results don't please you, then I'm terribly sorry, but I honestly had

117

no intention of swaying his decision in your favour.'

'Didn't you?' he demanded derisively, his glance insulting as it swept over her. 'You didn't perhaps think that, since you've failed to fulfil your obligations as a wife, you might try and make up for it in this way?'

She drew a sharp breath, controlling the tremor of pain and anger that shook through her. 'I'm afraid that my conscience did not dictate my actions, just as yours seemed not to have dictated your actions this evening.'

'And what's that supposed to mean?'

Melanie backed away involuntarily as he took a threatening step towards her. 'When you slipped away into the garden with Delia this evening, you were seen.'

'Ah! ... so that's it!' he smiled, but the smile did not reach his cold eyes.

'You at least have the decency not to deny it,' she stormed at him.

'Why should I deny it?'

'I don't suppose you stopped to consider that I might have been humiliated in front of everyone, and that they must have found it strange to think that, after being married only two weeks, you couldn't wait to be alone with your ... your ...'

'Mistress?' he filled in cynically. 'Is that the word you're looking for?'

'Yes,' she snapped, wincing inwardly as she recalled the conversation she had overheard on the terrace.

'You don't deserve any consideration from me, Melanie. You haven't earned it, and until you do ...' he hesitated, his expression hardening considerably, 'you'll just have to accept the situation as it is.'

'I won't be blackmailed into bed with you, Jason,' she remarked tritely after a reflective pause.

'Would you allow me to use other methods of persuasion?'

His eyes glittered dangerously as he reached for her,

but she stepped back swiftly. 'Don't touch me!'

'Afraid I might succeed?' he mocked her ruthlessly, and the colour surged into her cheeks as she recalled how easily she had succumbed to his lovemaking before.

'Isn't one conquest in an evening enough for you?' she spat out in self-defence, but she could have bitten off her tongue the next instant when the air between them positively crackled electrifyingly.

'Don't push your luck too far, Melanie. I've been very patient with you, but I have my limits,' he said menacingly, the muscles in his jaw bulging with the obvious effort to control himself. 'Goodnight!'

Melanie was angry, and had been hurt too deeply to pay much heed to Jason's warning that night, but she had cause, a few days later, to recall it with more than a little alarm.

'I'm so glad you could make it,' Adrian said as they sat facing each other over a cup of tea at the Carlton the Tuesday afternoon. His glance slid over her pale pink suit, and he smiled warmly. 'You look lovely.'

'Thank you,' she replied coldly, determined not to be sidetracked from the purpose of this meeting. 'There's something I want to discuss with you.'

'You look terribly serious, my sweet.'

'It's a serious matter,' she told him firmly. 'It's about your meeting with Barnaby Finch.'

Adrian paled visibly, his freckles standing out like beacons on his lean face. 'You know?'

Melanie nodded. 'It was a despicable thing to do, Adrian, and I shudder to think what will happen if Jason ever finds out that the one person he's always been able to entrust with confidential matters has let him down.'

'I'm sorry about that, but I couldn't help feeling that you'd been forced into marrying Jason Kerr,' he explained apologetically, 'and I considered I was acting in your own interests.'

'Well, I wish you hadn't.'

Adrian frowned down at his tea for a moment before meeting her direct gaze once more. 'How did you find out?'

'Barnaby confessed. He's that kind of person, and it troubled him to know that he'd been disloyal. I just hope he has the good sense not to confess to Jason as well.'

'Melanie, I'm sorry—I really am.'

'You ought to be!'

His hand touched her across the table. 'Am I not going to be forgiven?'

His expression was rueful, like a small boy who had been caught stealing biscuits, and her anger melted away.

'I've always valued your friendship, Adrian, but there's a limit to what one will tolerate from one's friends,' she reprimanded him gently.

'It won't happen again, Melanie, I promise.' His hand gripped hers firmly. 'Just look at me and tell me honestly—do you love your husband?'

Melanie hesitated momentarily, searching her own heart for the answer, but, despite everything she knew about Jason, her feelings still remained the same. Her love was strong enough to overcome whatever obstacles there might be, she realised as she sustained Adrian's glance and said quite calmly, 'You have no right to ask me something so personal, but if it will make you cease your senseless prying then, yes . . . I do love Jason. Very much,' she added convincingly.

Adrian went curiously pale as he saw the truth in her eyes, and his lips tightened. 'I envy him.'

'Adrian!'

He shook his head and looked away. 'I'm sorry, but it's the truth.'

Melanie's heart twisted. She hated having to hurt him, but there was nothing she could do about it, except perhaps not see him again and, making up her mind, she pushed back her chair and picked up her handbag.

'Thank you for the tea, Adrian.'

'Don't go yet,' he protested, gripping her wrist.

'I must.'

'What time does Jason get home?'

'He . . .' She bit her lip and relented. 'Well, he won't be home for dinner this evening. He's working late.'

'Have dinner with me?'

'I can't.'

'Just to show there are no hard feelings,' he persisted, and after a moment of thought she found herself agreeing to his suggestion.

'I would like to have dinner with you, Adrian, but I must be home before seven-thirty.'

'Whatever you say,' he smiled agreeably.

He drove her to a small restaurant he knew of, where they served meals throughout the day and night and, despite her misgivings, she enjoyed his company. It was quite like old times, having dinner with Adrian, and she was reminded of the many occasions they had been out together before Jason Kerr had walked into her life, disrupting her peaceful existence, and plunging her into a marriage that could only end in heartbreak.

She shook off her thoughts and tried to concentrate on Adrian, but Jason's hard features intervened, his steel-grey eyes accusing her, and filling her with guilt. There was no earthly reason for her to feel guilty about anything, she told herself, but she was more than just ordinarily relieved when Adrian eventually drove her home.

'When do I see you again?' he wanted to know when he unlocked the penthouse door for her and followed her in.

'I don't think it's wise for us to meet too often,' she tried to put him off gently.

'Melanie——'

'You've always been a dear friend, Adrian,' she intervened swiftly, 'but our friendship must end now that I'm married.'

'You're right, of course,' he admitted readily with a hint of sadness in his eyes as he framed her face with his hands. 'Take care of yourself, my sweet.'

He kissed her gently on the lips, and not for one moment did she think of resisting him. It was a kiss without passion; a kiss between friends who knew the time for parting had come.

'Am I interrupting?'

Startled, Melanie thrust Adrian from her, and she went cold with fright as she stared at her husband's thunderous expression.

'Jason!' His name passed her lips as she searched frantically for something to say, but Adrian was the first to recover from the shock.

'Good evening, Mr Kerr,' he said calmly, extending his hand towards Jason. 'I'm Adrian Louw, an old friend of Melanie's.'

'Indeed?' Jason remarked coldly as if he had never heard of him before and, ignoring Adrian's hand, he asked, 'Were you on your way out?'

'Well ... yes,' Adrian replied hesitatingly, dropping his hand self-consciously to his side.

'Then don't let us detain you.'

There was uncertainty in Adrian's glance as it met Melanie's but, sensing the suppressed violence in Jason, she said quickly, 'Goodbye, Adrian.'

Adrian hesitated only briefly before turning and striding towards the lift, but Jason did not wait to see him enter it before closing the door and locking it firmly. The entrance hall was suddenly too small to accommodate both Jason and herself, and Melanie turned towards the living-room, entering it on shaky legs, with Jason following close behind her.

The silence between them was deadly, and fear knotted her stomach as she stood watching him remove his jacket and tie, and flinging them on to a chair with an impatient, jerky movement before he approached her with a look in his eyes that chilled the blood in her veins.

'I could strangle you,' he muttered through clenched teeth, and his voice grated along her nerves.

'Jason, I can explain,' she began, backing away from him.

'I'm sure you can,' he laughed, but his laughter was more frightening than anything she had experienced before.

'That kiss didn't mean anything,' she protested, her heart leaping into her throat as he reached her with one lithe movement.

His arm imprisoned her against the hardness of his body, while his free hand gripped her hair, jerking her head back painfully as he forced her face into the open, and her eyes smarted as she looked up into his dark, angry face. There was no sign of mercy or leniency in the harsh contours of his features, and she knew somehow that it would be hopeless trying to reason with him while fury raged through him like a violent storm.

'I don't take kindly to someone trespassing on my property, and that freckle-faced youth was doing exactly that,' he spat out the words.

'I'm not your property,' she argued hotly, struggling against him, but her efforts merely served to make her more aware of him, of his strength, his muscular thighs against her own, and the roughness of the hair on his chest where his shirt had somehow come undone.

'You're mine, Melanie, whether you like it or not,' he

said thickly, pinning her hands behind her back while he undid the buttons of her jacket and slipped it off her shoulders despite her frantic struggle to restrain him. 'I've taken about as much as I can stand from you,' he added, his mouth hot and passionate against hers as he silenced her protests.

Her skirt slid to the floor, then, without taking his mouth from hers, he lifted her in his arms and carried her through to the darkened bedroom. She pummelled his chest with her fists, calling him all the names she could think of when he set her on her feet beside the bed, then a scream tore passed her bruised lips as the flimsy straps of her underwear gave way beneath his hands. With one swift movement she was stripped completely, her skin gleaming white in the moonlight filtering through the window as Jason thrust her unceremoniously on to the bed and pinned her down with his body.

He was breathing heavily, his anger fanning his desire, and his hands moved roughly over her body, punishing her rather than caressing, but her limbs weakened against him treacherously even as her mind begged frantically, *Not like this! Not in anger!*

'Jason, wait!' she pleaded, wrenching her mouth from his and gasping for breath.

'I've waited long enough,' he said hoarsely against her throat, foiling her attempts to escape from beneath him by pinning her arms at her sides.

'No! Don't!' she begged desperately, fear mingling with an intoxication she fought against as his mouth raked along her neck, leaving behind a trail of fire as he sought the fullness of her breast. A terrifying weakness invaded her body, bringing helpless tears to her eyes as she sobbed brokenly, 'Jason, please don't do this to me.'

'Shut up!' he grunted, silencing her eloquently with his mouth.

Tears poured unheeded down her cheeks until she could taste their saltiness in her mouth. Every part of her being rejected his brutality. She could not deny that she loved him and wanted him, but not like this—not in anger—and not with the sole purpose to punish.

Jason raised his head suddenly and leaned across her to switch on the light.

'My God!' he exclaimed, a look of disgust on his face as he stared down at her. 'If there's one thing that doesn't appeal to me, it's making love to a woman who's weeping at the thought of losing her virginity.' He rolled away from her and pulled on the shirt he had discarded, tucking it into his pants as he stood observing her with narrowed eyes while she dragged the bedspread over her naked, shivering body. 'Or is it perhaps that you're just plain scared I might find out you've lost your virginity already?'

If he had struck her he could not have inflicted more pain, and she flinched as she stared up at him speechlessly through a blur of tears while a hot wave of shame and humiliation swept through her, making her wish at that moment that she were dead.

'That's not true!' she cried chokingly, then she rolled over, burying her hot face in the pillow, and a few seconds later Jason slammed the bedroom door behind him with such a force that the windows rattled.

She remained where she was for some time, almost as if she were afraid to move, but, as the outer door slammed shut, a sure indication that Jason had gone out, her shoulders began to shake, and she wept silently into her pillow.

Her eyes were still red-rimmed and swollen in her pale face when she emerged from the bathroom an hour later, and she felt decidedly shaky as she went through to the kitchen to make herself a strong cup of tea. She stared at her distorted reflection in the stainless steel kettle, and decided grimly that her life had become just as distorted since she had married Jason. Nothing seemed to make sense, and she could understand herself least of all. In his anger he had wanted to take possession of her and, loving him as she did, she could not accept the brutal way in which he had attempted it. If the circumstances had been different; if there had been gentleness in his approach, she would not have been able to resist him, she realised weakly, and her treacherous body tingled at the thought.

'Oh, God,' she moaned softly, burying her face in her trembling hands. 'I should hate him, but I can't. I want only to love him, but I daren't, and I don't know what to do about it.'

When she finally stopped shaking she drank her tea and went to bed, but she slept fitfully all night, and awoke the next morning after eight to find that Jason had already left for the office.

Relief mingled with regret as she changed into a warm pair of slacks and a sweater, and knee-high boots. She brushed her hair vigorously until it shone like pure gold, and applied a little make-up before going through to the kitchen to pour herself a glass of orange juice. A cold slice of toast was all that remained of the breakfast Jason had prepared for himself and, helping herself to it, she walked through the living-room and out on to the roof garden.

The sun was shining weakly through the smog, but the breeze had a sting to it, and it whipped a little colour back into her cheeks. She did not sit down, but leaned against the wall of the penthouse as she ate her toast and drank her orange juice. Her eyes turned involuntarily in the direction of Greystone Manor, and she longed suddenly for the stability and safety of the home she had offered up so much for.

Swallowing down the remainder of her breakfast, she went through to the study and telephoned Barnaby to come and fetch her. When the doorbell chimed a few minutes later, she glanced at her watch in surprise. It could not possibly be Barnaby, unless he had suddenly sprouted wings, and it was also too early for the people who serviced the penthouse daily, she decided, frowning as she lifted the latch of the front door.

Delia's elegant presence on the doorstep came as something of a shock to Melanie, and she stared at her stupidly for a moment.

'Melanie, my dear, may I come in?' she asked sweetly and, without waiting for an invitation, she stepped inside, her expensive perfume filling Melanie's nostrils.

'I was actually on the point of going out,' Melanie told her defensively, wondering distractedly as to the purpose of this unexpected visit.

'I haven't much time at my disposal either, but I'm sure you could spare me a few minutes,' Delia smiled with deceptive warmth, and Melanie felt a shiver of apprehension crawl up her spine.

'If it's something important . . .'

'It's important to me, yes,' Delia insisted, walking through to the living-room as if she owned the place and subsiding elegantly into one of the chairs. She crossed her shapely legs and waited for Melanie to seat herself before she explained. 'I thought we might get to know each other better. After all . . .' she smiled complacently, '. . . we do have something in common, don't we?'

'You mean Jason, of course.'

'Quite right,' Delia admitted, studying her perfectly manicured nails. 'He'll never be a faithful husband, you must know that.'

Melanie was instantly on her guard. 'I never imagined he would be.'

'It doesn't concern you?'

'No,' Melanie lied, controlling her features. 'Should it?'

Delia's beautifully arched eyebrows rose a fraction

higher. 'I must say that's an extraordinary attitude to adopt, but perhaps it's just as well. That way you won't get hurt.' With one graceful movement she was on her feet. 'Oh, well, I would have loved to stay a while longer, but I must be on my way, darling ... and do return this to Jason.' She dropped a gold cigarette lighter on to the table, and Melanie, who had risen in the process, felt her legs begin to shake beneath her as Delia explained. 'He left it at my apartment last night. 'Bye for now.'

There was a look of triumph on Delia's face as she let herself out. She had scored a hit, and she knew it. Melanie picked up the lighter and clutched it in her hand. Jason's initials were engraved on it, leaving her in no doubt that it was his. She closed her eyes for a moment as she tried to assimilate the shattering knowledge that Jason had sought solace in Delia's arms. It was to be expected, she supposed, but it hurt none the less. It hurt so much that it was like a physical pain lodging in her chest, and she sat down quickly on the chair she had vacated as her limbs gave way beneath her. Delia had every reason to be triumphant. She had predicted that Jason would return to her, and it had happened almost sooner than she herself might have expected. What hurt Melanie most was the despairing knowledge that she had driven him into Delia's arms.

She fought back the hot tears that stung her eyelids, and just in time too, for Barnaby arrived a few minutes later to take her out to Greystone Manor. She pulled herself forcibly together, put the lighter away in the drawer of her bedside table, and chatted to Barnaby as if nothing had happened, but the pain of her discovery lingered with a determination she could not shake off.

Sister Wilson's shrewd glance took in Melanie's pale and drawn features, but she remained silent, and Granny Bridget had sunk too deep into her own world to notice any change in her granddaughter's appearance.

It was the unhappiest day Melanie had ever had to live through, and her grandmother's drastically declining health added to the load she had to bear. She spent the day up in her grandmother's bedroom, seated beside her chair in order to massage some warmth into her cold hands, and listening with growing concern to her meanderings into the past. There was no longer any sign of the proud, sometimes defiant old woman she had known, and she cried silently in the garden when Sister Wilson finally insisted that her grandmother should rest.

'She's had a long and happy life, Melanie,' Sister Wilson comforted her when they had a moment together before Barnaby arrived to collect her. 'Your life is only just beginning,' she added wisely.

'How can I seek my own happiness while Granny Bridget——' Melanie's voice broke, and she swallowed with difficulty, determined not to cry in front of this efficient-looking woman.

Sister Wilson pushed Melanie into a chair and frowned down at her. 'This may sound callous to you, my dear, but don't allow your own happiness to slip through your fingers because of your concern for your grandmother.'

'It would be inhuman and quite impossible for me not to be concerned,' Melanie protested indignantly.

'It would be even more inhuman if your marriage suffered a severe blow as a result of it.'

Melanie stiffened. 'What do you mean?'

'I'm not a fool, Melanie,' Sister Wilson said sharply. 'You've been married only a few weeks, and instead of blossoming into a radiantly happy woman, you've become pale and drawn. Come to think of it,' she added thoughtfully, 'the last time I actually saw you looking really happy was before your father's death.'

'You're exaggerating,' Melanie remarked defensively, but as Sister Wilson shrugged and left her alone in the living-room, she admitted to herself silently that it was the truth.

She tried to recall when last she had laughed, and found she could not remember. She was seldom amused by anything these days, and summoning a smile was fast becoming an effort she could do without. There was nothing really to laugh about. Everything had become so dreadfully serious that tears were becoming more natural than laughter.

'Oh, what's the use of wallowing in self-pity?' she asked herself fiercely, and went in search of Sister Wilson to tell her that she would wait in the garden for Barnaby.

He arrived a few minutes later and they drove back to the city in silence, almost as if he sensed her need to be alone with her thoughts.

'Having to cart me around like this is a nuisance, isn't it?' she said sympathetically when he dropped her off.

'Not at all,' he assured her hastily. 'It's nice to get away from the office at times, especially on a day like today.' He snapped his fingers so loudly that he succeeded in making her jump. 'I almost forgot—the boss said to tell you he'll be working late this evening. The final contract with Steel Incorporated must be ready for signing tomorrow.'

Melanie nodded thoughtfully, but her mind was on something else. 'You said something about getting away from the office on a day like today. What did you mean?'

'The boss is in a rare mood today,' Barnaby informed her with a rueful grin. 'We all try to keep out of his way when he's on the warpath, but some weren't so lucky and a few heads have rolled as a result.'

So Jason was in one of his rare moods, was he? she thought wryly as she took the lift up to the penthouse. Did the hours he had spent with Delia the previous evening not come up to scratch, or was he still fuming because of the innocent kiss she and Adrian had exchanged? It was something worth thinking about, and she would certainly have plenty of time to think during the lonely hours ahead of her that evening.

Melanie made a light supper for herself and watched the television for a while, but she lost interest half way through the programme and switched it off. She stood about restlessly, played records for a time, and finally decided to go to bed with a book. In theory, the latter was a good idea, but in practice she found herself unable to concentrate on the printed page before her.

She put the book aside after another attempt to concentrate had failed, and switched off the bedside light. She intended to be asleep when Jason returned, but she was still awake when she heard his key in the door shortly after ten. Her heart thumped wildly as she heard his footsteps approaching her door, but he walked on past her room to his own without stopping.

She shrank lower beneath the covers, her body tense and alert to every movement he made. Cupboard doors opened and closed, and a few minutes later she could hear him taking a shower in the bathroom across the passage. Then everything was quiet; so quiet, in fact, that the thudding of her heart sounded like a bass drum in her ears. She was nervous and edgy, and she could not think why, but a light tap at her door a few minutes later told her why.

Ignoring his knock, she almost held her breath as she lay hoping frantically that he would go away, but the door opened and the passage light shone into the room, silhouetting his tall, broad-shouldered frame. She closed her eyes tightly, pretending to be asleep, but the hammering of her heart seemed loud enough to give her away. She remained perfectly still, hardly daring to breathe, then she heard the door being closed softly.

Relieved that her ruse had worked, she sighed audibly, and the next instant the bedside light was switched on.

'I had a feeling you were awake.'

Her nerves vibrated with shock as she stared up at Jason, her wild glance taking in his lean, clean-shaven cheeks, the dampness of the dark hair flecked with grey at the temples, and the blue towelling robe which left a section of his tanned, muscular chest bare.

The aura of sensual masculinity that hovered about him was overpowering, stirring her senses in a way she was beginning to know so well and, clutching at the covers for protection, she raised herself up against the pillows and demanded unsteadily, 'What—What do you want?'

His glance was faintly amused as it followed the distinct outline of her body beneath the covers, almost as if he were recalling to memory every part of her as he had seen it the night before, and a hot wave of shame and embarrassment swept through her.

'Don't look so stricken, Melanie,' he said at last, and the springs of the bed gave way beneath his weight as he sat down beside her. 'I only want to talk to you.'

'What about?'

'Anything and everything,' he shrugged nonchalantly, taking a cigarette from his cigarette case and frowning down at the packet of matches in his hand.

'Use this,' she said, unable to suppress the flicker of triumph as she removed his cigarette lighter from the drawer and handed it to him.

'Where did you find it?' he asked, staring at it in surprise as he turned it over in his hand.

'Delia returned it this morning.'

'I see.' His expression was unfathomable as he lit his cigarette and pocketed the lighter. 'Aren't you going to demand an explanation?'

'No.'

'It didn't upset you to find out that I'd gone to her straight from you?' he demanded with mocking incredulity, and she looked away.

'No.'

'You're lying!' he accused sharply, putting out his newly lit cigarette and imprisoning her with his arms on either side of her.

'All right!' she snapped, her body tense as she fought against the effect his nearness had on her pulse rate. The clean, musky smell of his body invaded her nostrils and stirred her senses, making her intensely aware of him as a man, and of her own vulnerability. 'All right,' she said again, swallowing with difficulty. 'It was humiliating to discover that—that when you had no success with me you rushed at once to her waiting arms, and Delia found great satisfaction in letting me know where you'd been.'

'Did she imply that I'd made love to her?'

'No,' her hands clutched agitatedly at the sheets, 'but why else would you have gone there if it wasn't to— to——'

'I didn't,' he said quietly, capturing her wary glance. 'Didn't what?' she asked blankly.

'I didn't make love to her.'

'You surely don't expect me to believe that?'

'If I can believe that there was nothing but friendship in that kiss I witnessed last night, then why can't you believe that I didn't make love to Delia?'

Melanie looked away. 'You didn't believe last night that Adrian's kiss was innocent.'

'I was angry at the time.' His fingers gripped her chin,

forcing her to look at him. 'Did I frighten you last night?'

His compelling glance wrung the truth from her, and she whispered, 'Yes.'

'Is that why you cried?'

'You came to your own conclusions about that, remember?' she reminded him, still wincing as she recalled his remarks centred on her virginity.

'Melanie ...' His fingers slid across her cheek and beneath her hair at the nape of her neck. 'Have you never said anything terrible in a moment of anger?'

'Of course I have,' she admitted breathlessly, a weakness invading her body at his touch.

'Then you must understand what had prompted me to say what I did?'

She nodded, unable to speak as his hand slid across her shoulder and down the length of her arm. He raised her hand and pressed his warm lips against her palm, then against her delicate wrist where her pulse throbbed wildly, and finally against the hollow of her elbow.

'You're trembling,' he accused softly, and then his lips found hers.

Melanie raised her hands instinctively to ward him off, but her palms encountered the warmth of his hair-roughened chest, and lingered where she could feel the heavy beat of his heart quite distinctly. She tried not to respond, forcing herself to think of Delia, but his mouth moved backwards and forwards against hers with a sensuality that made her body tingle deliciously. Her lips finally parted beneath his and, to her dismay, she was kissing him back with a hungry yearning that seemed to rise from an over-full heart to fill her entire being.

As he sensed her response, his kisses became urgent with rising passion, and Melanie found herself without the strength to fight against the weakness which invaded her limbs.

'I want you, Melanie,' he groaned, his hand moving urgently against her back as his lips sought the hollow beneath her ear with devastating effects.

Her breath came jerkily over parted lips, and she whispered his name, hovering on the brink of confessing her feelings.

'You're not going to send me away, are you?' he demanded persuasively, sliding the strap of her nightdress off her shoulder to leave the way clear for his conquering lips.

'I ... oh, Jason ...' she moaned softly, suspended between fear and ecstasy as his mouth gently explored the curve of her breast. 'Jason, I—I've never slept with a—a man before,' she confessed haltingly, completely unaware that she was caressing his chest and smooth shoulders in the most encouraging way.

'I know,' Jason grunted, stretching out a hand and plunging the room into darkness.

Her heart leapt into her throat as she felt him shrug himself out of his robe and get into bed beside her. His arms reached for her, gathering her against him with surprising gentleness, but, to her dismay, she discovered that the only thing between them was her flimsy nightdress, and this, too, he was removing with a dexterity which she knew was born of experience.

Resentment surged through her, and she tried to resist him, but as she felt the heat of his muscular body against her own, her resistance melted away beneath the onslaught of her own emotions. His lips and hands explored her body with an intimacy she had never known, arousing her to an instant and passionate response that sent a flame of desire pulsing through her veins. There was no longer any room for coherent thought, and she was beyond caring that Jason's actions were motivated by desire only. She loved him, and that was all that mattered; that, and the driving need to surrender herself to him completely. She clung to him blindly, allowing him to guide her with urgently whispered commands until she experienced the shatteringly ecstatic sweetness of fulfilment, and later, as she lay drowsy and contented in his arms, she knew that she would remember this night with a tenderness and awe for the rest of her life.

CHAPTER EIGHT

As the city awakened to a new day Melanie stretched and stifled a yawn. She became aware of an unfamiliar weight lying across her body, and her eyes flew open to discover Jason lying on his back beside her with his left arm flung across her. She stared at him for a moment, unable to grasp what he was doing in her bed, and then, as she remembered, her lips curved into a tender smile.

She looked down at his arm lying across her and noticed for the first time the scars Barnaby had mentioned. She fingered them lightly, almost lovingly, then something made her turn her head to find Jason observing her with an amused expression on his face.

To cover up her confusion, she said: 'Why didn't you tell me the truth about that lion you killed?'

'I gather Barnaby has been talking out of turn,' he remarked without resentment.

'Well, when I mentioned the lion which I presumed you had shot, Barnaby corrected me,' she replied defensively, glancing at him through lowered lashes. 'It was a pretty wonderful thing to do, saving a man's life like that.'

'There was nothing wonderful about it,' he said abruptly. 'It was an act of self-preservation. Because it was suffering, the lion was in a foul mood. It was either him or us.'

'I still think it was a wonderful thing to do,' she insisted adamantly, but she found she still could not look at him when he raised himself up on one elbow and gazed down at her.

'You look like a little girl this morning with your hair lying all over the pillow,' he said softly with a hint of sensuality in his voice as he changed the subject. 'I think I'm in need of confirmation that you're the woman I made love to last night.'

She stared at him for a moment, digesting his suggestion, then she sat up with a jerk and, realising that she did not have a stitch of clothing on, she fell back against the pillows, dragging the covers about her as she did so.

'My dear Melanie, there's not a part of your delectable body that isn't known to me after last night,' he reminded her mockingly, and her cheeks flamed.

'You're a brute!' she accused him, but her accusation ended in a gasp of surprise when the sheet was flung aside. She made a wild grab at it, but he had removed it beyond her reach, and covered her instead with his own body.

A delicious weakness assailed her limbs as she felt that hard, sinewy body above her and, when his hand cupped her breast, she locked her hands behind his head and raised her lips unashamedly for his kiss, but Jason held back tantalisingly.

'I'm a brute, am I?' he demanded, watching the play of emotions on her sensitive features with a look of triumph in his eyes.

'Sometimes, yes,' she insisted, her breath quickening with each caress. 'You give with one hand, but make very sure that you take with the other.'

'Isn't that what life is all about?' he mocked her before lowering his head and claiming her lips at last, and she gave herself up to the ecstasy of the moment until a more pressing thought came to mind.

'Jason ...' she began, determined to ignore the sensations created by his mouth exploring the column of her throat until she had satisfied her curiosity. 'You went to Delia's flat with the intention of making love to her, didn't you?'

'Yes.'

He nibbled lightly at her ear, sending a shiver of delight through her, and she raised her hands to ward him off as she asked, 'Then why didn't you?'

'I realised, in time, that it would only diminish the sweetness of my victory over you,' he laughed softly and triumphantly as he brushed aside her hands and continued to explore the smooth warmth of her shoulder. 'And last night was worth waiting for,' he added sensuously.

'Was that all it meant to you? A victory?' she asked, barely able to conceal her disappointment.

'Should it have meant something more?'

'No, I suppose not, but——'

'You talk too much,' he accused harshly, covering her mouth with his own, and no matter how much she tried to resist, her body had a will of its own, and it responded eagerly to the demands he was making on her.

Later that morning, when Jason had gone to the office, she mulled over the events of the past two days, and a new fear took possession of her. Loving him as much as she did, what was she going to do when Jason finally decided it was time to end their marriage?

She tried to picture her life without him, and shuddered at the emptiness she visualised. Nothing would be quite the same again after knowing and loving Jason Kerr.

The telephone rang while she was preparing a late breakfast for herself and, thinking it was Jason, she almost ran to answer it.

'I wanted to telephone before this, but I was out of town yesterday,' Adrian's voice came over the line, and Melanie swallowed down her disappointment. 'Are you all right, Melanie?'

'Yes, of course I'm all right,' she said a little abruptly as she guessed the reason for his concern.

'Was Jason very angry?'

'He was, but I managed to explain the situation without delving too deeply into the facts.'

She crossed her fingers at her little white lie, but Adrian accepted it without question.

'I'm glad,' he sighed. 'I wouldn't like to think that because of my actions he——'

'Forget it, Adrian,' she interrupted hastily in a reassuring voice. 'It was a kiss between friends, and Jason has accepted it as such.'

'I don't suppose I'll see you again,' he said at length, and went on to explain, 'I've been transferred to Cape Town on promotion, and I'm leaving at the end of the week.'

His news came as something of a shock, but she was glad for his sake. 'I hope you'll be very happy there, Adrian.'

'Thank you.' He hesitated, almost as if he had wanted to add something and then changed his mind. Then he said hurriedly, 'Well, goodbye, Melanie, and everything of the best.'

The line went dead before she could reply, and she replaced the receiver a little sadly. Another chapter in her life would end with Adrian's departure, and soon there would be no one left but Jason.

'Jason,' she whispered his name despairingly. He had plucked her ruthlessly from her peaceful existence, not caring how he had disrupted her life, and he would discard her just as ruthlessly when she had served her purpose.

Shaking off her morbid thoughts, she planned something special for dinner that evening, and went down to the shops with her list. She had to keep herself occupied, she told herself fiercely, or go mad thinking of the lonely future she visualised for herself.

The telephone rang for the second time that day shortly after five-thirty, and Jason's voice came clearly over the line.

'I want you to come down to the basement, Melanie.'

Alarm quickened her pulse rate. 'Is something the matter?'

'Something *will* be the matter if you don't come down here at once,' he said impatiently.

'I'll be there in a few seconds,' she assured him, and replaced the receiver.

Hurrying through the kitchen, she untied her apron from her waist and turned down the temperature of the oven. Fortunately the dinner would not spoil, and she could serve it at any time when Jason was ready, she told herself as she locked the front door behind her and took the lift down to the basement.

She tried to imagine what could be wrong. Jason had made his request sound so urgent, and her thoughts ran wild eventually with images of Jason being injured in some way and unable to get himself up to the penthouse on his own. She was close to panic when the lift doors slid open and, rushing out blindly, she collided with a solid masculine chest, and felt strong hands steadying her.

'Jason?' she gasped, clutching at him anxiously as her eyes searched his immaculately clothed body for some sign of injury. 'Are you all right?'

His heavy eyebrows rose above cold, unfathomable eyes. 'Don't I look all right?'

'Yes, but——' She choked back the words which threatened to cascade from her lips and took a deep breath to steady herself. 'You made it sound so urgent that I should come down here at once. I thought ...'

'You thought something had happened to me?' he filled in for her a little incredulously.

'Yes.' She swallowed with difficulty and lowered her glance to his striped tie while she tried to regain her composure.

'No one has ever been concerned about me before,' he said softly, his warm breath fanning her forehead. 'This is a unique experience.'

The sudden desire to slide her arms inside his jacket in order to press closer to him was very strong, and she moved away from him jerkily. 'Why did you want me to come down here?'

'I have something to show you.'

Taking her hand in his strong fingers, he drew her towards a small red Triumph parked beside his silver-grey Jaguar, and her heart thudded uncomfortably as she glanced up at the man beside her.

'Jason?'

'It's yours,' he said abruptly, his keen glance sweeping her face.

Melanie felt a little sick at heart when she touched the gleaming red body of the Triumph lightly with the tips of her fingers. 'It's a lovely car, but——'

'It's quite fast, too, so you'll have to be careful when you drive it,' Jason interrupted, taking a small bunch of keys from his pocket and unlocking the door on the driver's side.

'I can't accept it, Jason.'

Her statement seemed to hang suspended in the air between them during the ensuing silence, and her slim body stiffened as he turned to glance at her coldly.

'Why not?' he demanded abruptly.

'I already owe you a considerable amount of money.'

His hands sliced the air impatiently. 'That has nothing to do with this.'

'It has *everything* to do with it,' she protested unhappily.

'Melanie——'

'I can't, Jason,' she interrupted him hastily, fighting

back the tears that rose unbidden to her eyes. 'It's extremely kind of you, but I can't accept it. Please, I——'

'Melanie!' His hands gripped her shoulders and he shook her slightly. '*Forget* about that money owing to me.'

'Forget about it?' she asked incredulously in a voice that shook. 'How can I forget about it when it's the reason for our marriage?'

'*One* of the reasons,' he corrected abruptly.

'Yes, one of the reasons,' she acknowledged bitterly, realising that none of the reasons for their marriage had anything to do with love. 'Oh, Jason ...' she whispered tiredly, resting her head for a moment against his chest almost as a gesture of defeat.

'Come on,' he said impatiently. 'I want you to try out the car.'

'Jason ...'

'I insist!'

There was a clash of wills as their eyes met and held, but Melanie finally gave up the struggle and did as she was told.

Jason climbed in beside her and she drove through the city, unconsciously taking the road out to Greystone Manor. Despite everything, she enjoyed the feeling of being in control of such a powerful little car, and the drive, begun so reluctantly, became an unexpected pleasure.

'Does she handle all right?' Jason asked as they left the city behind them.

'Beautifully,' she was forced to admit.

'Pull off the road just ahead there,' he suggested and, as she parked the car beneath the trees and switched off the engine, he turned to face her. 'Have I tempted you yet to accept my gift?'

The corners of her mouth quivered with the effort not to smile, and looking straight ahead, she said: 'I suppose I can't expect Barnaby to continue playing chauffeur whenever I want to go somewhere, and you're against my using a bus, so ...'

'You're seeing sense at last.'

She looked at him then, and frowned. 'I'm trying to find a good excuse for my acceptance so that I won't feel so bad about it.'

Jason undid the restraining seatbelt and leaned towards her. 'You know, you intrigue me.'

'Do I?' she asked, keeping her voice casual as he placed his arm along the back of her seat behind her shoulders.

'I've never known a woman yet who's had to find an excuse for accepting a gift from me. They usually say thank you very nicely, and accept it as if it had been my duty to bring them something.'

'I don't think I would be able to tolerate any gift if it was given out of a sense of duty.'

'No, I didn't think you would.' He tilted her face up to his. 'Do I get a thank-you kiss?'

She raised her lips innocently, intending to kiss him lightly, but his hand slipped beneath her hair at the nape of her neck, and held her there. His kiss deepened, became intense and demanding and, without really knowing what she was doing, she undid the catch of her restraining seatbelt and pressed closer to him. Nothing seemed to matter when she was in his arms like this, and she welcomed the emotions aroused by his caresses, for they drove away her fears and doubts until they were of no significance.

She trembled against him, returning his kisses with a mounting passion until he groaned softly and released her.

'I think it's time we went home, don't you?' he suggested, and the sensuality in his voice made the blood leap wildly through her veins.

She nodded without looking at him and, after restoring some order to her clothes, she fastened her seatbelt with trembling hands and drove back to the city in silence.

Melanie was never quite sure during the next few weeks exactly where she stood with Jason. He could be painfully aloof at times, and passionately tender on other occasions. It was confusing and frustrating and, although she knew he would have no qualms about throwing her out the moment he grew tired of her, she could not prevent herself from hoping that, in some way, she might make him care just a little.

They attended several functions at which Delia Cummings was also present, and although Jason made no visible effort to encourage her flirtatious behaviour, he made no effort to discourage her either. It was inevitable that the newspapers would begin to speculate about them, and some even went so far as to suggest that the affair between Jason and Delia had never ended. This infuriated and humiliated Melanie, but she dared not say a word for fear of giving herself away in the process. It would be the final humiliation if Jason should discover that she had been fool enough to fall in love with him.

'I saw your grandmother today,' he told her unexpectedly one evening as he strolled into the bedroom after taking a shower.

With nothing but a towel wrapped about his lean hips, he looked frighteningly masculine, and her senses stirred in response.

Angry with herself more than with him, she turned her back on him and snapped, 'Were you checking up to see how long you would still have to wait before claiming what's due to you?'

'That was uncalled for!'

His voice had the effect of a whiplash, and she winced inwardly. 'I'm sorry.'

'I went to see your grandmother because I happen to

like her, and because I thought it would look strange if I showed no interest in her welfare,' he explained smoothly as if nothing had happened, 'but since you've brought up the subject of money, there's a little matter I want to discuss with you.' She tightened the belt of her gown nervously as he came up behind her. 'What did you do with that cheque I gave you for personal expenses?'

Her body stiffened. 'Why do you want to know?'

'It hasn't gone through the bank yet.'

'Oh.'

He swung her round to face him, his hands scorching her through the silky material and making her embarrassingly aware of the fact that she had nothing on underneath.

'What did you do with it, Melanie, or do I have to shake the truth out of you?'

With her eyes on the wide expanse of his bare chest, she whispered, 'I tore it up.'

Jason released her almost as if she had stung him. 'Would you mind telling me why?'

'I have enough money of my own, and I didn't feel that I had the right to accept more from you.'

'You're my wife, Melanie.'

She shrugged with affected carelessness and turned towards the dressing table, her hands idly rearranging her personal effects displayed on it as she said quietly, 'I'm your wife only until my father's debt has been repaid, or when you get tired of me—whichever comes first.'

His fingers gripped her wrist and her brush fell on the floor as he jerked her round to face him. 'You're still my wife, and until such time as I throw you out, you will accept an allowance from me whether you like it or not. Do I make myself clear?'

'You can't force me to accept it, Jason,' she persisted, ignoring the danger signals as she raised her head proudly and met his angry glance undauntedly.

'Would you like to bet on that?'

His voice was dangerously calm, but the fingers that gripped her wrist bit into the soft flesh.

'You're hurting me!' she gasped as the pain shot up her arm.

'I feel like thrashing you,' he said through tightly clenched teeth, and she was jerked against him with such a force that the breath was almost knocked out of her body.

His kiss was a punishment she was forced to endure, but it lasted only a few seconds before she felt the anger drain from him and passion take over. It happened so swiftly that it caught her off guard, and her desire rose to match his with an intensity that surprised and delighted him.

Lost in the turmoil of her emotions she had no idea when and how he had removed her gown, but it lay in a silken heap about her feet where his towel joined it a few moments later and, with his mouth against hers, he lifted her in his arms and carried her towards the bed.

'You're the most infuriating woman I've ever met,' he said eventually when the emotional storm had passed and they lay quietly beside each other in the darkened room.

'But you still want me,' she replied with an audacity that surprised even herself.

Jason laughed softly and slid his hand possessively over the flat of her stomach. 'You're damn right, I still want you.'

'The question is, for how long?'

'Who knows?' he sighed. 'A few months, maybe a year, but you'll have to be something exceptional to last longer than that.'

He kissed her briefly on the lips and rolled away from her, but the insensitivity of his remark had been like the thrust of a sword, and she fought against the tears as she lay staring into the darkness. She glanced at his dark shape beside her in the bed and longed to touch him, but he had erected that invisible barrier between them which robbed her of the freedom to succumb to the desire.

'Jason . . . ?'

'Mm . . . ?'

'Have you never loved anyone?'

He was quiet for such a long time that she was beginning to think he had not heard her, then he switched on his bedside light and turned over, leaning on his elbow as he stared down at her.

'What makes you ask that?'

'I just wondered,' she replied with forced casualness as she narrowed her eyes against the brightness of the light. 'Have you?'

'I believe I've come close to it, but love has no place in my life.' He smiled derisively as her eyes widened in surprise. 'Does that shake your romantic little heart?'

'Yes,' she said tritely, veiling her eyes with her gold-tipped lashes. 'I believe that everyone needs to love and be loved at some time or another, and if that makes me a romantic at heart, then I don't deny it.'

'I prefer to look at life realistically,' he argued coldly. 'Desire is a very down-to-earth emotion which most people can understand. To desire someone is one of the basic human needs.'

'Desire is like a log fire,' she added softly, loving his nearness and longing for the strength of his arms about her. 'When the fire has burnt out there's nothing left but ashes. It can't last for ever.'

'Nothing lasts for ever,' he said harshly, turning on to his side once more and switching off the light.

'Jason . . . ?'

'Go to sleep!' he ordered sharply, and Melanie lapsed

into silence, unable to do as she was told, but not daring to say another word.

The sound of his regular breathing eventually told her that he had followed his own advice, but it was only when, some time later, he rolled over in his sleep and flung an arm across her waist that she went to sleep herself.

Jason announced without warning the following morning that he was flying down to Cape Town on business.

'When will you be back?' she asked as she stood aside miserably and watched him pack a small suitcase.

'I should be back on the early morning flight tomorrow, but I'll be going straight to the office,' he said abruptly, fastening the catches of his suitcase before turning to raise her face to his. 'I won't see you again before tomorrow evening.'

He kissed her lightly on the lips, then he was gone, leaving her with the most frightful sensation that he had just walked out of her life for good.

The silence in the penthouse was oppressive and, making up her mind hastily, she packed an overnight bag and drove out to Greystone Manor.

Flora's dark face beamed as she let Melanie in, delighted at the news that she would be staying the night, but in Granny Bridget's room Melanie found a worried Sister Wilson hovering beside her grandmother's bed. She assured Melanie that there was nothing to worry about, but later in the day Dr Forbes had to be called in, and Melanie knew, somehow, that the end was very near for her beloved grandmother.

Dr Forbes, who had been their doctor for so many years, shrugged helplessly when Melanie confronted him.

'I've done everything I possibly can,' he said quietly, and Melanie nodded silently as she accompanied him to the door. 'I would stay the night, if I were you, Melanie,' he added almost as an afterthought. 'Sister Wilson may need your help.'

'I brought an overnight bag with me,' she told him, and he nodded approvingly as he turned and walked towards his car.

Melanie had never felt so desolate before in her life. There was nothing more to be done now, except wait, and the long vigil beside Granny Bridget's bed began.

Granny Bridget opened her eyes again late that afternoon and looked directly at Melanie seated beside her. For a moment her expression looked blank, then it cleared partially, and her lips moved as though she were trying to say something. Melanie leaned closer, placing her ear almost against her grandmother's lips in order to catch the words.

'Jason will take care of you,' she heard her grandmother whisper tiredly. 'You must love him well.'

Melanie replied unsteadily in the affirmative, and her grandmother sighed contentedly. The cold hand of fear clutched at Melanie's heart as she glanced anxiously at Sister Wilson. 'Is she——?'

'She's resting again,' Sister Wilson assured Melanie quietly, but Granny Bridget never opened her eyes again.

As the hours dragged by, Melanie's body began to ache with weariness as a result of sitting so quietly in the straight-backed chair beside the bed with her grandmother's hand in her own. She arched her back carefully, trying not to draw attention to herself, but Sister Wilson's shrewd eyes noticed her discomfort.

'Why don't you get some rest, Melanie? I'll call you if there should be a change in her condition.'

Melanie shook her head adamantly. 'Thank you, but I would prefer to remain where I am.'

The older woman shrugged and hovered over

Granny Bridget for a moment while she checked her pulse, then she resumed her seat and the vigil continued.

It was a night Melanie knew she would never forget for as long as she lived. During the long hours there was plenty of time to think, but her thoughts were incoherent and too painful to linger on. She stared at the sunken eyes and cheeks of the old woman lying on the high bed, and found it almost incredible to believe that this was her grandmother, the woman who had been like a mother to her for so many years. A film of tears clouded her vision, but she blinked them away hastily and arched her aching back once more.

Just before dawn the following morning, Granny Bridget sighed heavily, and then there was a deathly silence in the room.

'She's gone, my dear,' Sister Wilson said calmly after a brief examination, confirming Melanie's worst fears. She raised the sheet over Granny Bridget's peaceful features and touched Melanie's arm. 'Come downstairs with me, I must let Dr Forbes know.'

Melanie allowed herself to be led away from the room and was thankful for the blessed numbness which seemed to strip her of every vestige of emotion at that moment.

Left alone in the living-room, she drew aside the curtains and watched the sky gradually change from a velvety black to grey. The sun would rise on another day, she thought distractedly, but in her heart there was a dark void; an emptiness that she hardly dared think about. Now that Granny Bridget had gone, she had no one except Jason, and soon he would not want her either.

'Love him well,' she recalled her grandmother's words, and the recollection sent a searing pain through her bruised heart.

'Dear God,' she whispered, clutching at the heavy drapes as the watery sun rose above the tree tops. 'The trouble is, I love him *too* well.'

At the sound of approaching footsteps she made an effort to pull herself together, succeeding only partially as she felt the room sway about her.

'Dr Forbes will be here any minute now,' Sister Wilson informed her.

'What's the use?' she choked on the rush of tears. 'She's *dead*.'

'He's coming all the same.' Sister Wilson glanced at her sharply and stepped forward to take Melanie's arm. 'Sit down, my dear, you look dreadfully pale.'

'I'm fine, I——' The room tilted dangerously, and she clutched wildly at the hands that tried to steady her as a blanket of darkness threatened to descend upon her. 'I think I'm—going to faint,' she whispered incredulously, and then the darkness enveloped her completely.

The living-room was bathed in sunlight when she opened her eyes again and tried to focus on the anxious faces of Dr Forbes and Sister Wilson.

'What—what happened?' she demanded, trying to struggle into a sitting position, but Sister Wilson pushed her back against the cushions on the sofa.

'You fainted, remember?'

'Oh … oh, yes.' Melanie passed a tired hand over her eyes as she recalled clutching at Sister Wilson moments before she had blacked out, and she was suddenly consumed with embarrassment. 'That was silly of me. I'm sorry.'

'It often happens in the early stages of pregnancy,' Dr Forbes smiled at her reassuringly over the rim of his spectacles as he closed his medical bag.

'In the—what?' Melanie asked faintly, praying frantically that she must have heard him incorrectly.

'Didn't you know?' he asked a little incredulously.

'I—I had no idea. I——' She broke off suddenly, realising foolishly that the signs *had* been there, but she had been too preoccupied to give it much thought. Now, as the implications of her dilemma hit her with a shattering force, she almost wished herself back into oblivion as she buried her face in her hands and moaned, 'Oh, no, *no*!'

Sister Wilson's arm was about her shoulders instantly. 'I think we should telephone your husband and ask him to come over.'

'No!' She sat up quickly, fighting against a renewed bout of dizziness as she glanced up at the two people staring down at her. 'Jason was in Cape Town yesterday, and most probably won't be back yet. I'll be perfectly all right, and—I must ask you both not to mention a word of this. I—I don't want Jason to—to know about—about the baby yet.'

'If that's what you want, Melanie, you can count on our silence,' Sister Wilson assured her hastily, glancing at Dr Forbes. 'Not so, doctor?'

'Certainly,' he nodded, looking as though he was not quite sure what he was agreeing to, but, if it made Melanie happy, then that was all that mattered.

Dr Forbes departed soon afterwards, but not before issuing instructions that Melanie was not to drive her car until her dizziness had departed. Flora diffidently served breakfast in the dining-room, shaking her head and clicking her tongue in sympathy and distress at the death of her mistress, but Melanie merely toyed with her food, and ate nothing.

Her sleepless night had left dark smudges beneath her eyes, and an uncommon tightness about her usually soft mouth. Her grief was too great to allow her to shed tears at that moment, and her thoughts were in too much of a chaotic state to make any rational decisions. She struggled with a deep sense of loss, as well as the certain knowledge that Jason would be horrified if he should learn about the child she was carrying.

'Haven't you eaten your breakfast yet?' Sister Wilson asked as she returned to the dining-room after making a few telephone calls.

'I'm not hungry,' Melanie whispered, pushing her plate aside. 'Have you——?'

'I've made all the necessary arrangements,' Sister Wilson assured her hastily, then she frowned. 'When are you going to let your husband know … about your grandmother, I mean?'

Melanie pushed her fingers through her untidy hair and sighed. 'I'll go home first to wash and change, then I'll take a drive down to his office and—and break the news to him.'

Sister Wilson stared at her thoughtfully. 'He came to see your grandmother quite a few times during the past weeks. Did you know that?'

'No, I didn't.' Melanie was too tired to be surprised. Besides, nothing Jason did surprised her any more. She gestured vaguely and asked, 'What are you going to do now?'

'Oh, I'll take a short holiday, and then start looking for another job,' the older woman told her almost casually, but Melanie glimpsed an expression in her eyes that told her Sister Wilson was not as unaffected by Granny Bridget's death as she pretended to be, and a little bit of warmth stole into her cold heart.

'Will you stay on here until we've made the necessary arrangements with regard to the servants and the house?'

'Of course, my dear,' Sister Wilson smiled a little sadly. 'They'll be heartbroken at the thought of leaving. They've been here so long.'

'I know.'

'Now that there's a baby on the way, you must think

of making a home for it, and the penthouse isn't exactly the most suitable place for a child.' She observed Melanie closely. 'Do you think you and your husband might come and live here at Greystone Manor?'

'I ... don't think so.' Melanie looked away uncomfortably, then back again at the woman seated opposite her. 'Sister Wilson, I—I would like to thank you for everything you did for Granny Bridget.'

'Don't thank me, my dear.' She reached across the table and clasped Melanie's hand briefly. 'It was a pleasure to have been a part of your family for so long.'

Melanie collected her overnight bag and her coat from the hall closet, and, taking her leave of Sister Wilson, she drove carefully back to the penthouse and took a refreshing bath to alleviate her tiredness.

She selected a plain russet-coloured woollen dress and zipped herself into it, then sat down in front of the dressing-table mirror and tried to do something about her appearance. She brushed her hair vigorously, bringing it back to its natural silky sheen, but no amount of make-up would conceal the deep shadows beneath her eyes. She stared hard at herself, but it felt as though she were looking at a stranger. Her face was pale and pinched, but it was the unnoticeable change in her that distressed her most.

Without being conscious of her actions, she placed her hands against her flat stomach. She was going to have Jason's child, and suddenly she no longer dreaded the thought. When Jason had no further need of her, she would have his child to fill the lonely void.

He must never know, she decided, picking up her handbag and taking a last critical look at herself in the mirror. Jason must never know! The last thing she wanted was that he should feel under an obligation to continue with their marriage. She could not bear to have him on any such terms.

CHAPTER NINE

THE tall building which housed the offices of Cyma Engineering stood etched against the clear wintry sky, and Melanie stared up at it for a moment, recalling the first time she had entered through those sliding glass doors. She had had no idea then of the enchantment and bitterness which lay before her, just as she had no idea at that moment how Jason would receive the news she to impart to him.

'Melanie!' A hand touched her arm lightly, and she found herself looking up into Barnaby's laughing eyes. 'This is a surprise, having the boss' wife pay us a visit.'

'It's good to see you again, Barnaby,' she said with a tight smile, avoiding the penetrating curiosity of his glance. 'Is Jason in?'

'Sure,' he said abruptly, accompanying her to the lift he had just emerged from and pressing the button to open the doors. 'Go on up.'

The lift glided upwards with well remembered speed, and Melanie clutched at the side railing to steady herself. Jason's secretary was not at her desk, but his door stood slightly ajar and, knocking briefly, she pushed it open further and stepped inside.

Delia was there, her slender body pressed close to Jason's, and her arms wrapped about his neck. Melanie's heart gave a sickening jolt, and then she froze, fighting against the rising nausea.

'Melanie!'

Jason frowned and disengaged himself hastily, but he remained where he was as their eyes met and held across the room. It was as if everything ground to a sudden halt inside of her, and the only clear thought that kept revolving through her mind was, 'I must not faint, or be sick. Not here—not now!'

'Darling, you look positively haggard,' Delia remarked caustically, draping her fur about her shoulders as if nothing unusual had happened. 'You really must do something about your appearance, my dear, if you don't want your husband's eyes to roam.'

'That's enough, Delia. Will you please leave us,' Jason said harshly without taking his eyes off Melanie's pale, thin face.

'But what about our luncheon appointment?'

'Some other time,' he snapped.

'Please don't let me interrupt your arrangements,' Melanie remarked coldly, recovering sufficiently to speak. 'What I have to say can wait.'

'No, it can't!' Jason moved with lightning speed as she turned to leave, and gripped her arm, forcing her to remain at his side. 'Close the door behind you, Delia.'

'But, darling——!' Delia pouted, her eyes flashing hatred at Melanie who stood silent and helpless beside Jason.

'We'll talk some other time, but right now I want to be alone with my wife,' he insisted harshly, indicating the door, and Melanie almost felt sorry for Delia when she saw the dull red colour surging into her cheeks.

'Oh, very well,' Delia agreed angrily and, picking up her purse, she swept out of the office and closed the door behind her with unnecessary violence.

Melanie flinched, her taut nerves reacting to the noise as Jason turned her to face him.

'You wouldn't have come here if it wasn't something important,' he said slowly, his eyes searching her face intently. 'Is it your grandmother?'

Melanie nodded, and her voice sounded cold and lifeless when she spoke. 'She died early this morning.'

'Did Sister Wilson let you know?'

Shaking her head, she disengaged herself and sat down in the nearest chair before her trembling legs gave way beneath her.

'I didn't fancy spending the night alone, so I drove out to Greystone Manor yesterday morning after you left for the airport. My grandmother was ill when I arrived, and Dr Forbes was called in.' She drew a shuddering breath as the incidents of the previous evening flashed vividly across her mind. 'Sister Wilson and I spent the night beside her bed.'

Jason's eyes flickered strangely. 'You were with her when she died?'

'Yes.'

'Why didn't you telephone me instead of driving out here when you must be half asleep on your feet?'

If only she *had* telephoned, Melanie thought despairingly, then she would not have seen . . . ! She pulled herself together and shrugged. 'I—I wanted to see you— to tell you personally, and not on the telephone.'

She stared at the tips of his polished leather shoes, refusing to meet his eyes, then he turned away and she heard him pouring something into a glass.

'Drink this,' he said calmly, bringing a glass of amber-coloured liquid into her line of focus.

'I don't really——'

'Drink it!'

It was a command, and she obeyed reluctantly, but her hand shook so much when she took the glass from him that she almost spilt some of the liquid on to her dress before she managed to get the glass to her lips. It was brandy, she realised, wrinkling her nose, but she obediently took a sip. It scalded her throat, but Jason placed his hand beneath the glass and forced her to drink more until she coughed and spluttered with tears streaming from her eyes.

'I've had enough,' she choked out the words, accepting his handkerchief to dab at her eyes.

He took the glass from her and placed it on the small table, then he sat down on his haunches in front of her, forcing her to look at him.

'I'm sorry, Melanie.'

'Why should you be sorry?' she demanded coldly. 'You can sell Greystone Manor now, and take what's owing to you. It's what you've been waiting for, isn't it? The opportunity to end our marriage so that you can return to Delia?'

Jason's expression became shuttered as he drew her to her feet. 'I'm taking you home. You need to get some rest.'

'I can drive myself.'

'I'm taking you, and your car will be sent over later,' he insisted, marching her from the office, past his secretary's desk and into the lift.

When they reached the basement of the building Melanie was almost thankful for his hand supporting her as she fought against the dizziness, and she was vaguely aware of him helping her into the Jaguar with unexpected gentleness. She shrank as far away from him as possible when he climbed in beside her, and they completed the journey home in silence.

'Take off your clothes and get into bed,' he ordered when they arrived at the penthouse, and Melanie was instantly rebellious.

'I'm not tired,' she snapped, but her breath caught in her throat when she found herself lifted high into his arms and carried into the bedroom as if she were a child. 'Let me go!' she cried when he set her down on her feet and tugged at the zip of her dress. 'What do you think you're doing?'

'I'm undressing you,' he stated quite calmly without desisting from what he was doing.

'No! Let me go!' she gasped, struggling against him, but tiredness overwhelmed her and he had no difficulty in stripping her down to her skin. 'I hate you! I hate you!'

'Yes, I know,' he announced in that infuriatingly matter-of-fact way of his as he picked up her frothy pink nightdress and helped her into it. 'I know you hate me,' he said again, 'but at the moment you're overwrought and tired.'

'You have no right to treat me like this! I'm not a child. I——'

She choked on a sob, and then her control snapped. Horrified at herself, but unable to do anything about it, she wept unrestrainedly while Jason lifted her on to the bed and pulled the covers over her. It was humiliating and degrading to cry in front of him like this, but it was some time before she was able to prevent the hot, scalding tears from paving their way down her cheeks.

Jason left her alone for a few minutes, giving her the opportunity to regain her composure, but when he returned she was unable to look at him.

'Feeling any better?' he asked, and the bed sagged beneath his weight when he sat down beside her.

'Yes, thank you.'

'Drink this,' he instructed quietly, offering her a glass of water and a small capsule which lay in the palm of his hand.

'What is it?'

'A mild sedative.'

'I don't want——'

'For God's sake, Melanie, allow me to know what's best for you at this moment!' The harshness in his voice almost succeeded in triggering off her tears once more, but she checked them forcibly. 'Drink it!' he ordered, ruthlessly determined to have his way.

Too tired to argue, she did as she was told and swallowed down the capsule.

'Now, close your eyes and go to sleep,' he ordered a little more gently, removing his jacket and tie, and lighting a cigarette.

She stared at him in surprise. 'What are you doing?'

'I'm going to sit here until I'm sure you're doing as you're told,' he said calmly, drawing deeply on his cigarette and blowing the smoke towards the ceiling.

Although part of her rejoiced at his presence, there was another part of her which strongly rejected the idea.

'If you hurry you could still be in time to have lunch with Delia,' she whispered, her eyelids drooping with fatigue.

Jason muttered something unintelligible and then said more clearly, 'Go to sleep! Forget about Delia!'

Forget about Delia! She could never forget about Delia, she thought as she drifted on the verge of oblivion, but her hand searched unashamedly for his, and as she felt the comforting pressure of his strong fingers about her own, she sighed and went to sleep.

Jason took over the arrangements for Granny Bridget's funeral with his usual flair for organisation and efficiency for detail, but Melanie was secretly grateful to him for doing so. Sister Wilson left Greystone Manor immediately after the funeral, but everything else remained as it was with the servants still in attendance.

Jason's plans for the future still remained a mystery to Melanie. She never questioned him, and he never mentioned the subject, but it was there between them like an impenetrable barrier keeping them apart, and increasing the tension and strain in the already faltering relationship. The knowledge of her pregnancy was a carefully guarded secret which she longed at times to share with him, but she dared not, and the effort of keeping silent began to gnaw away at her nerves.

They were invited one evening to the home of the

McAlisters to celebrate their daughter's coming of age. They could not decline the invitation despite Melanie's strange reluctance to attend and, shortly after their arrival at the McAlisters' exquisitely beautiful home, she realised the reason for her initial reluctance. Delia Cummings was there, draped elegantly in a glittering crimson gown, and Melanie knew with painful certainty that she could never hope to compete with someone so beautiful.

They acknowledged each other's presence with a cool nod, but with thirty-odd guests crowding the living-room and spilling out on to the terrace, no one noticed anything amiss. Melanie tried not to act the jealous wife by keeping an eye on Jason but, to her disgust, she found herself searching for his tall figure among the guests every few minutes.

The McAlisters' daughter, Susan, drew Melanie's attention. She looked so vitally alive that Melanie envied her secretly and, as their eyes met across the room, the slender, titian-haired girl excused herself from her friends and came to Melanie's side.

'I'm not very good at remembering names, but you're Melanie Kerr, aren't you?' she questioned in a friendly manner.

'Yes, I am.'

'I've heard so much about you from Mummy and Daddy. Especially Daddy,' she added with a smile. 'You made quite an impression on him.'

'I can't think why,' Melanie murmured selfconsciously.

'It's your freshness, your honesty and sincerity that he admired most, and now that I've met you, I can almost agree with him. You have that look about you that makes me realise why a man like Jason Kerr fell for you.'

'Oh.'

'Now I've embarrassed you,' Susan McAlister laughed. 'You must forgive me, Melanie, but we Mc-Alisters are inclined to speak our minds.'

Melanie could not prevent the smile that lifted the corners of her mouth. 'So I've noticed.'

'Your marriage really caused quite a stir among the people who knew Jason. The eligible women, especially, were quite put out, and I don't mind admitting that I was one of them,' Susan informed her without rancour as she directed her gaze across the room to where Jason stood talking to some of the men. 'He's really quite a handsome devil, isn't he?'

'I think so, yes,' Melanie replied truthfully, and without embarrassment.

'Oh, well, I'm a good loser, fortunately. Not like Delia,' Susan remarked, glancing curiously at Melanie. 'Did you know there's a possibility that she might accept an offer made to her by a Paris fashion house?'

Melanie's heart lifted expectantly, but she kept her voice casual as she said: 'No, I had no idea.'

'It will be the best thing for all concerned if she does accept the offer,' Susan said knowingly, glancing at Melanie's empty glass. 'Can I get you some more champagne?'

'No, thank you.'

Someone caught Susan's attention and she touched Melanie's arm lightly. 'You must excuse me, but I do hope I'm going to see a lot of you in future. I like you.'

Melanie stared after her thoughtfully. Susan McAlister was really quite incredible, but she could not help liking her frankness. She had certainly given Melanie something to think about, and she only hoped that Susan's information was correct. With Delia out of the way there might be a possibility that...!

She stopped her thoughts right there when she glimpsed Jason and Delia slipping out on to the terrace and disappearing into the shadows. So much for her hopes, she thought dismally. If Jason gave any indication that he wanted Delia to remain in South Africa, she would do so, Melanie realised, and there was no reason to believe that he would not ask Delia to remain.

The hopelessness of it all dogged Melanie's footsteps all evening, and when they arrived back at the penthouse she had made up her mind, irretrievably, about her future. To continue living in this uncertainty was driving her mad, and the sooner she put an end to it, the better.

Jason emerged from the shower with a towel wrapped characteristically about his lean hips and, for the first time since her grandmother's death, he entered her room. Shutting her mind and heart to his fatal attraction, she continued to brush her hair with quick firm strokes, but the thudding of her heart threatened to choke her. He stood behind her for a moment, but, when she refused to meet his eyes in the mirror, his hands touched her shoulders in a caressing gesture, and her treacherous body quivered in response.

'Melanie . . .'

'Take your hands off me,' she said coldly, lowering the brush and clutching it in her lap as if it were a lifeline.

'Why this unexpectedly chilly welcome?' he demanded mockingly as he drew her to her feet and removed the brush from her hand.

'I want my freedom, Jason.'

His eyes narrowed slightly, but his expression remained unaltered. 'What's the hurry?'

'I believe I'm just as entitled as you are to ask for my freedom when I want it.'

'No, my dear Melanie,' he shook his head slowly, his eyes lingering with undisguised pleasure on the clearly noticeable curves of her body. 'You'll get your freedom when I say so.'

His arms were locked about her before she could think of moving away and, as she felt the heat of his body through the thinness of her night attire, a familiar weakness took possession of her. Despising herself for feeling the way she did, she threw her head back and glared up at him.

'You can't force me to stay with you.'

'It's part of our agreement, remember?' he mocked her. 'You will continue to be my wife until I no longer wish it.'

'What kind of man are you?' she demanded breathlessly, struggling against him as he lifted her with effortless ease and carried her towards the bed. 'Can't you see that I don't want to stay with you any longer?'

His mouth twisted cynically. 'Don't you?'

'Let me go at once!'

He obeyed her unexpectedly, and she screamed involuntarily as she landed in a heap on the bed. She rolled away from him in an effort to escape, but he was beside her in an instant, pinning her down on to the bed with his leg across her thighs. Her wrists were gripped ruthlessly and, with her arms raised above her head, she was rendered utterly helpless. Devilish amusement lurked in his eyes as he observed the swift rise and fall of her breasts. She passed the tip of her tongue nervously across her dry lips and, noticing this, Jason lowered his head and captured the full moistness of her mouth with his own.

Her inability to curb her response made her want to weep. She was caught defencelessly in the web of her love for him, and she trembled against him as the passion of his kiss found a rising echo in her. Sensing this, he released her wrists and caressed her with the deliberate intent to arouse her. Clinging desperately to her sanity, Melanie tried to push him away, but her efforts were futile.

'You still want me just as much as I want you, and if

you deny it, then you're a rotten little liar,' he said, his breath warm against her lips.

'Jason, please . . .'

'Don't fight me, Melanie. You know you'll only get hurt,' he warned, his eyes darkening with desire as he buried his face in the enticing, scented hollow between her breasts.

Melanie could no longer control her clamouring emotions and, as her resistance crumbled, she laced her fingers through his crisp dark hair and cradled his head against her.

Melanie never discussed her desired freedom with Jason again, and neither did he mention it, but, as the days passed, an unnatural calm seeped into their relationship. It frightened Melanie, almost as if it were a premonition of something yet to happen. Every day she expected Jason to return home with the news that he had sold Greystone Manor, and for this reason she spent every available moment in her old home, sorting through personal items, and making a list of the things she wanted to keep. It was a painful task she had set herself, but it was something with which to fill the days when her thoughts drove her to despair.

She had sensed a change in Jason since that night she had demanded her freedom, and she had caught him several times observing her with watchful, brooding eyes. It unnerved her considerably, but she could find no reasonable explanation for his strange behaviour. It was possible that Delia's plans to leave the country might have something to do with it, but she preferred not to think so, although she could find no other palpable reason for his reticence.

While out shopping one afternoon she stopped at an enchanting little coffee bar for a break, and from her window seat she watched the passing traffic listlessly as she sipped the strong aromatic coffee she had ordered.

A swish of silk beside her table made her look up sharply to find Delia standing there, looking as though she had stepped out of a leading fashion magazine that very minute. Melanie's fine woollen suit was tastefully elegant, and quite without fault, but Delia always succeeded in adding a subtle touch of glamour to everything she chose to wear, and Melanie could not help but envy her.

'Darling, how delightful running into you like this,' that slightly husky but well-modulated voice exclaimed. 'Do you come here often?'

'No, this is the first time,' Melanie replied stiffly, instantly on her guard against this woman.

'What's the matter, darling?' Delia smiled sweetly, but there was a hint of venom in her dark eyes. 'Is your marriage not working out as well as you'd hoped?'

Melanie clenched her hands in her lap under the table. 'My marriage is working out perfectly, thank you.'

'You can't fool me,' my dear,' Delia laughed unkindly. 'The signs are there for everyone to see.'

'Signs?' Melanie questioned innocently.

'Strain, darling,' Delia enlightened her. 'It's written quite plainly all over your face.'

'Really?'

'You can't say I didn't warn you,' Delia reminded her carelessly. 'Jason just isn't the kind of man to be satisfied with one woman only, but fortunately I understand these little whims of his. Quite frankly, I give your marriage less than a month before he walks out on you. He's already showing signs of restlessness.' She smiled disdainfully and stepped away from the table. 'I must rush. Goodbye, darling.'

Melanie stared after her speechlessly as she left the coffee bar. There was no way in which she could have disputed Delia's statement even if she had had the opportunity to do so, and the fact that she was Jason's wife in no way gave her the confidence she desired.

A chauffeur-driven car drew up at the curb, and Melanie's heart almost stopped beating when she saw Delia step off the pavement and get into it. The man already seated in the back was obscured from Melanie's vision, but, as the car moved away, she caught a glimpse of a dark head close to Delia's.

Jason! she thought instantly, but she discarded the idea almost at once, admonishing herself severely for allowing her imagination to run away with her.

Collecting her parcels, she made her way back to the penthouse, but in the silence of those exquisitely furnished rooms she found her suspicions returning with agonising insistence. It *could* have been Jason, she told herself, but there was no way of knowing for sure unless...! Melanie pulled herself up sharply. What would it look like if she telephoned the office to check up on her husband? She could, of course, make up some excuse for telephoning if she found him in, she decided as she entered the study and stared uncertainly at the instrument on Jason's desk.

Biting her lip nervously, she lifted the receiver and stood with it in her hand while indecision churned through her. Then she made up her mind and dialled Jason's number.

'Mr Kerr's office, good afternoon?'

Melanie's heart lurched uncomfortably. 'Mrs Howard ... is my husband in?'

'I'm afraid not, Mrs Kerr. He went out to lunch and hasn't returned yet.'

'Oh.' Melanie swallowed heavily, clutching the receiver so tightly that her knuckles showed white.

'Shall I ask him to telephone you when he comes in?' Mrs Howard wanted to know in her warm, friendly voice, unaware that she had plunged Melanie into the depths of despair.

'No—no, that won't be necessary, thank you,' Melanie managed somehow. 'It—wasn't very important.'

She replaced the receiver and closed her eyes as she leaned against the desk for a moment. It was possible, then, that the man with Delia could have been Jason! She groaned and sank into the chair behind her, jealousy and suspicion tearing her apart.

'It *could* have been Jason,' she whispered her thoughts aloud, 'and there's every likelihood that it *had* been him, but—Oh God, don't let it be so!'

She jumped to her feet and paced about restlessly. She tried not to think, but her thoughts raced about uncontrollably, conjuring up visions of them together somewhere, of Jason making love to Delia. It was like the thrust of a sword to an open wound, and Melanie wrapped her arms about herself as if to ward off the pain.

It was no use, she told herself as she dashed away her tears with the back of her hand. She could not go on like this! She *must* make him see that it was futile to continue with this meaningless marriage.

'Love has no place in my life,' he had said once, and she could believe that now. He was incapable of loving anyone. Desire? Yes! But love? Never!

Picking up her coat and handbag, she walked out of the penthouse and roamed the streets until tiredness washed away her agonising thoughts. The increase in the late afternoon traffic told her that Jason would soon return home, but she could not face him yet. She had to have time to think about what she was going to say to him and, whatever it was, it had to sound convincing, she decided distractedly as she found a taxi and gave the driver Greystone Manor's address.

The smell of stale cigarette smoke hovered unpleasantly about her as she leaned back against the seat and closed her eyes. Heavens, she was tired! she thought as the taxi made its arduous way through the traffic and headed out towards her old home. It was the only place she could think of where she would find the peace and tranquillity she needed at that moment and, until Jason sold it, it still belonged to her.

She paid off the taxi and walked slowly up the drive. The sun was setting swiftly, and the chill in the air made her shiver. The garden always looked drab during the winter months when the trees had shed their leaves, and the lawns had been yellowed by the frost. In September everything came alive again as if by magic, and the seedlings would grow and flower in a glorious array of colours.

Melanie's eyes filled with sudden tears. Spring would come to Greystone Manor this year with strangers in residence, and there was nothing she could do to prevent it. Choking back the sob that rose in her throat, she turned and ran lightly up the steps to the heavy oak door. Alarmed, she stared at it. She had not brought her key with her!

Despondently, she leaned against the door and then, pursing her lips, went down the steps again and round to the back of the house. Her only hope now was to find one of the servants about to obtain the key to the back door, but the padlocks on the doors of the servants' quarters told her that they had gone to their respective homes.

She could willingly have burst into tears at that moment, but that would not have solved her problem. Her eyes searched for a possible way to enter, and then she saw it. The pantry window was small and high, but if she could lift the old-fashioned catch as she had done once before as a child, she could climb through it and get into the house that way.

Shifting an old drum to beneath the window, she tested its steadiness and climbed on to it. She searched her handbag for something sharp and flat, and decided ruefully that it would have to be her nail file. She struggled for several minutes before she finally managed to release the catch and, lifting the window, swung her legs over the sill and dropped to the floor as lightly as she could.

It was a most undignified entrance, she thought grimacingly, but she was inside the house at least, and not outside in the cold. She closed the window and walked through the kitchen. Everything was clean and in its proper place, she noticed, but she hurried on down the long passage and into the living-room. She found matches on the mantelshelf, and lit the fire, kneeling in front of it to seek a little warmth.

When the room had warmed up, Melanie went back to the kitchen to make herself something to drink. The house was silent, but it was not an unfriendly silence. It soothed, rather than disturbed, and when she returned to the living-room with her mug of coffee, she was considerably calmer than when she had arrived, she realised as she shed her coat and made herself comfortable in front of the fire.

She had allowed her imagination to run away with her, but facts and fantasies had mingled to create a painfully disturbing picture. She had to decide what to do about her future, and the future of the child she was expecting. One thing she was very sure of—she would not allow Jason to take the child from her, and she would not remain his wife because of it!

Coldly, and almost clinically, Melanie set aside her emotions as she began to analyse the situation. She loved Jason, but there was no future for her with him. He had told her quite categorically on several occasions that he would give her her freedom as soon as he tired of her and, according to Delia, that day was approaching swiftly. During the three months they had been together he had never once given her any indication that he cared for her in the slightest way. He was gentle, yes—even tender at times, but the barrier of aloofness was there each time to prevent her from getting too close to him. 'Keep away', was the unspoken command his attitude conveyed, and she had not dared to trespass for fear of being humiliated.

As darkness descended on Greystone Manor, Melanie switched on a small reading lamp and returned to her chair by the fire. What was Jason doing? she wondered. Would he be unduly concerned to arrive home and find her not there, or would he shrug off her absence as unimportant?

Her thoughts did not hurt her at that moment, and it seemed to her as if she had gone beyond the point where anything would ever succeed in hurting her again.

She must have fallen asleep there in the comforting warmth of the fire, but an hour later she stirred and opened her eyes to find Jason looking down at her from his great height. Her heart leapt to her throat as she observed his grim expression in the subdued light, but her fascinated attention was caught and held by something else. Jason was wearing a light grey suit, and her befuddled mind now recalled him sitting down to breakfast in it that morning. The man in the back of the car with Delia had been wearing a dark suit, so it *couldn't* have been Jason after all.

Relief swept through her like a tidal wave, but she controlled herself hastily. There was too much that still had to be said between them, but, to her dismay, she found that she had no idea where to begin, or how to make him understand that she could no longer continue living a life of uncertainty with him.

CHAPTER TEN

'I THOUGHT I'd find you here, but when I discovered you'd left your key behind, I telephoned all over the place without success before taking a chance on finding you here after all,' Jason told her grimly, warming his hands by the fire. 'How did you get in?'

'I climbed in through the pantry window.'

Jason's eyebrows rose sharply as he turned to face Melanie. 'That was rather dangerous, wasn't it?'

There was something strange about Jason; something that kept her seated in her chair in the curled up position he had found her in as she replied haltingly, 'I . . . came here on the spur of the moment. The servants had already gone, so I . . . climbed in through the window.'

'I see.' He paced the floor restlessly, looking about him as if he were seeing Greystone Manor's rather drab living-room for the first time. 'You love this place, don't you.'

It was a statement, not a question, and Melanie's curious glance followed him as she said; 'Yes, I do.'

'It could do with extensive renovations.'

'I know,' she admitted, staring wistfully into the fire. 'I had plans to do something about it myself . . . once.'

What's the matter with me? she asked herself angrily. Why don't I say what I have to say to him and get it over with?

'Would you like to live here again?'

His question jolted her back to life and sparks of anger flashed in her eyes as she stared at him across the room. 'You know that's out of the question.'

'It's not impossible, you know,' he said, coming towards her into the circle of subdued light, and she was suddenly aware of that dangerous magnetism that reached out to enfold her.

'You're talking in riddles,' she accused sharply, intent upon fighting this fatal attraction which could only lead to more bitterness.

'Perhaps this will make sense.'

A bulky envelope was dropped into her lap, and she stared at it as if hypnotised without touching it. She had a vague idea as to the contents of the legal-looking envelope, but was too afraid to open it.

'What is it?' she heard herself ask hoarsely.

'It's the title deeds of Greystone Manor.'

She raised her lashes to reveal incredulous blue eyes. 'I don't think I understand.'

'Your father's debt no longer exists as far as I'm concerned, so I'm giving your family home back to you.' Jason smiled briefly in that arrogant, self-assured manner she so often hated. 'There's one condition, though.'

Melanie stiffened. 'And that is?'

'That we stay together . . . for better or worse.'

Her pulse drummed against her temples at his arrogant supposition that she would fall for his suggestion. To agree to it was an incredible temptation, but his cold-blooded proposal was not enough for her hungry heart, and she rose to her feet, clutching the envelope in her hands as she walked away from him into the shadows.

'Do you always have to resort to emotional blackmail to get what you want?' she asked quietly, but her insides were shaking uncontrollably.

'It's one way of making sure that I do get what I want, and it's never failed me in the past.'

She steeled herself against the stab of pain as she

swung round to face him. His attitude, where he stood with his back towards the fire, was that of a man who was used to having his own way, and who was prepared to go to any lengths to ensure it. She had known this from the moment they had met, and she had accepted it in the past, but at that moment she could not tolerate it. She had never felt more like doing him a physical injury, but she drew a ragged breath to steady herself and walked slowly towards him.

'You astonish me, Jason,' she said coldly, stopping directly in front of him and raising her angry eyes to his. 'I don't think I've ever met anyone like you before, and I hope I never shall again.'

His eyes narrowed perceptibly. 'What do you mean by that?'

'Much as I love this old house, I'm giving it back to you to do with as you wish,' she said quite clearly, thrusting the envelope back at him as if it were something distasteful.

'Do you realise what you're doing?' he asked incredulously, looking unusually pale beneath his healthy tan.

'Yes, I know what I'm doing,' she said stiffly, clenching her hands so tightly at her sides that her nails bit into her soft palms as she sustained his glance. 'I'm refusing to be pressurised into continuing our marriage. You held the whip hand when Granny Bridget was still alive.' Her voice broke unexpectedly, but she controlled it with an effort, and continued, 'I now claim the right to choose what I shall do with my future, and you can't deny me that any longer.'

As they faced each other in silence, Melanie thought she had never seen Jason look so unsure of himself before, and all at once she knew she could not bear to see him like that. His arrogance and abominable self-assurance had angered her many times, but it was preferable to seeing him stripped of his confidence. Her heart softened as she saw him lower his eyes to the envelope in his hands, but something held her back and, in that fraction of a second, he looked up again, and there was a frightening determination in the set of his jaw.

'All right!' he said abruptly, and she stepped back involuntarily as he flung the offending envelope across the room. It landed with a dull thud on the floor, but Melanie paid no attention to it as she stared up at Jason with renewed interest. 'Without making use of emotional blackmail,' he continued in a voice that sounded quite unlike him, 'would you consider continuing with our marriage?'

'I might,' she admitted, her receptive heart quickening.

'Melanie...?'

His strong, beautifully shaped hands gestured in an unconsciously pleading way, but she knew she had to ignore their silent appeal if they were to reach a complete understanding.

'My answer would depend on several things.'

'What, for instance?' he demanded abruptly, thrusting his hands into his pockets almost as if they had offended him.

'Where does Delia fit into this arrangement?'

There was a brief, agonising silence before he said: 'Nowhere, as far as I'm concerned.'

She glanced at him through lowered lashes, hating herself for what she was going to ask, but determined to get at the truth. 'Are you asking me to remain your wife because you've heard that Delia might be going away?'

'Don't be ridiculous!' he accused sharply. 'I made it quite clear to her the other evening at the McAlisters' home that I wanted to have nothing more to do with her in future, and that was *before* I heard of her plans to leave for Paris.'

'I see . . .' she whispered softly, finding balm in his statement for her aching heart.

Jason took a step towards her, his wide shoulders blotting out the firelight as he stood looking down at her. He raised his hands as if to touch her, then let them fall to his sides again.

'You mentioned that your answer would depend on several things. What are the others?'

Her heart was racing at a suffocating pace as she asked, 'Can you give me any reason why I *should* agree to stay with you?'

He stared at her searchingly for a moment before he turned away and stood contemplating the log fire with that brooding expression she had observed so often lately. The line of his jaw looked taut, and his shoulders moved slightly beneath the superb cut of his jacket, giving Melanie the curious impression that he was fighting a private battle with himself. An eternity seemed to pass before he turned to look at her, and she knew suddenly, from the wariness of his expression, how much it had cost him to say simply,

'I need you.'

Speechless with happiness, she could only stare at him, but Jason had reached the end of his endurance as he bridged the gap between them with two quick strides and gripped her shoulders.

'For God's sake, Melanie, don't just stand there! Say something!'

She could feel his hands shaking, but she was afraid to accept what he was saying. She had to be sure, she decided as she asked jerkily, 'For how long will you need me? Just until someone else takes your fancy?'

'I suppose I deserve that,' he groaned, releasing her.

'You told me yourself that I would have to be something—something exceptional to last longer than a year,' she persisted, close to tears as the bitterness of the past months flowed from her lips.

'My God!' he exclaimed, passing a shaking hand over his smooth dark head.

'Nothing lasts for ever, remember?' she added, wincing inwardly at the well-remembered pain of his callous remarks.

'All right,' he said hoarsely, gesturing her to silence. 'I don't deny that my past is a little unsavoury, but if the truth is the only thing that will convince you, then you're going to get it.'

Her trembling legs would no longer carry her weight and she lowered herself on to the arm of a chair as Jason removed his jacket and tie, and lit a cigarette.

'I wanted you from the moment I saw you standing beside your father's grave,' he said roughly, pacing the floor like a caged animal while he spoke. 'I wanted you, but I knew it wouldn't just be a case of whisking you off to my bed. With you it would have to be something more. When we met, after the funeral, I realised fully how different you were from the women I'd been used to, and I was more determined than ever to have you. I hadn't quite planned what I was going to do when you yourself gave me the solution.' His steely glance encompassed the room before it settled on her once more. 'You loved this old house but, more than that, you wanted to shield your grandmother from yet another shock. You really had no choice but to agree to marry me, and although marriage had never entered into my plans before, I consoled myself with the idea that divorce was easy. When you eventually began to bore me, we could go our separate ways.'

It hurt to hear him speak like that, and she gestured pleadingly, but he ignored her with ruthless determination.

'Things worked out a little differently,' he went on,

his lips twisting cynically. 'I found myself thinking of you at odd times during the day and night, which is something that had never happened to me before. I wanted you very much, but instead of taking what was rightfully mine, I found myself agreeing to give you time to adjust because, for some reason I couldn't explain even to myself at the time, I didn't want to frighten you.' He drew hard on his cigarette and flung the remainder into the fire with an angry gesture that disturbed her. 'The crunch came that night when I stormed out and, like an idiot, went to Delia's flat.'

'Jason——'

'I couldn't touch her,' his confession stopped her, and she almost cried out with pain at his tortured expression. 'I knew then that, even if I could never have you, I could never touch another woman again as long as I lived, and I knew for sure how I felt about you that day you walked into my office to tell me about your grandmother and found Delia there.'

'You were going to have lunch with her,' she reminded him gently.

'Yes,' he admitted, stopping beside her chair and staring down at her broodingly with his hands thrust deep into his pockets. 'It had become imperative that I should make her understand it was all over between us, and I finally got that opportunity at the McAlisters' home.'

Melanie realised now that her suspicions had been unfounded when she had seen them disappearing into the shadows of the garden that night, but she remained silent.

'After the party that night, I tried to talk to you,' Jason interrupted her thoughts, 'but you'd turned into a little spitfire, demanding your freedom. I realise now, of course, that you must have seen Delia and myself doing a disappearing act, but your behaviour wasn't very encouraging at the time, so I decided to shelve the discussion until the tension between us had eased a little. When I arrived home this evening and found you weren't there, I knew something had to be done, and quickly, if I didn't want to lose you.'

'So you came armed with the title deeds as your guarantee of success,' she could not prevent herself from adding.

Jason flinched as if she had struck him, but he sustained her glance, questioning what he saw in the depths of her eyes for the first time.

'Melanie?'

'Did it never occur to you that just the slightest sign that you cared would have been enough persuasion?' she asked shakily.

'What are you saying?' he demanded softly, his wariness incredibly touching for a man who was always so sure of himself.

Making no effort to control the tremor in her voice, she said: 'You don't have to buy my love with Greystone Manor, Jason. I would gladly forsake my old home to spend the rest of my life with you if that's what you really want.'

She was in his arms then, tasting the salt of her tears on his lips. He kissed her with such infinite tenderness that she clung to him in rapturous delight, returning his kisses with a hungry yearning she no longer had to keep in check.

It was some considerable time before they came down to earth and, lifting her in his arms like a child, Jason sat down in the large armchair beside the fire and cradled her on his lap. Melanie buried her face against his shoulder, at peace with the world as he held her and caressed her with a gentleness that was awe-inspiring. To be near him like this, to know that this sometimes formidable and self-possessed man needed her, was almost too incredibly wonderful to take in all at once.

'I know I've said a good many things over the past three months to make me appear a crass, unfeeling swine, but ...' He placed his hand beneath her chin and brought her face out into the open. 'I love you, Melanie. God help me, but I do, and that's something I've never said to any woman before.'

Melanie thought for a moment that her heart would burst with happiness, and she raised her hand to stroke his cheek tenderly as she had wanted to do so often in the past.

'Jason, are you sure?'

'Very sure,' he said, turning his lips into the palm of her hand before he kissed her hard and satisfyingly on the mouth. 'Melanie, I'm not an easy man to live with—you must have realised that already. I'm selfish and possessive.'

'And arrogant, and ruthless,' she added, flinging her arms about his neck with an abandon that surprised even herself. 'Oh, darling! I love you so very much, and I went nearly out of my mind when I thought you could never love me too.'

'I've been a brute to you, haven't I?' he asked seriously, and she smiled up at him tremulously.

'Sometimes, yes,' she admitted, raising her lips for his kiss.

His arms tightened about her, and tenderness made way for passion. Their hands fumbled with buttons, seeking a closer contact as their emotions sharpened on desire, but it was Jason who drew back a little for a moment of sanity.

'Perhaps I should explain,' he said, burying his face in her corn-coloured hair. 'My parents were never a wonderful example of marital bliss. They never made any secret of the fact that they both indulged in affairs from time to time, and their constant bickering drove me out of the house at a very early age. There was no such thing as love, my father once told me, and I believed him. My studies and my job became my entire life, and with success came women. None of them ever meant anything.'

Melanie was silent for a time as she digested this shattering information, then she said softly, 'Delia must have meant something to you. Everyone seemed to think you would marry her.'

'I might have married her eventually, I suppose, if I hadn't met you,' he admitted, brushing his lips against her closed eyelids. 'In you I found what I'd subconsciously been searching for, but it took some time for me to realise exactly what you meant to me. I hope you're listening,' he added mockingly after a brief pause, 'because I most probably shan't ever repeat all this to you again.'

'I'm listening,' she assured him contentedly, 'and I'm making a mental record of every word you're saying so that, no matter what happens, I shall always remember this wonderful moment in my life.'

'You silly child,' he laughed, kissing her briefly. 'I suppose you'll like to come and live here in your old home?'

She nestled closer to him, listening to the heavy beat of his heart. 'Only if *you* want to.'

'You could have the place redecorated as you've always wanted to,' he suggested generously.

'Oh, yes,' she sighed, a secretive little smile hovering about her lips. 'I would like our children to grow up here at Greystone Manor as I did.'

Jason laughed softly as he gazed down at her with a teasing look in his eyes. 'Having children is something I haven't thought about yet, but I dare say I'll get used to the idea in time to be able to tolerate the little brats.'

Melanie coloured slightly and buried her face against him. She could not delay her news for a moment longer. 'You'll have to get used to the idea very quickly, I'm afraid.'

'Melanie?' His hand stilled on its caressingly destructive path along the hollow of her back. 'You're not serious.'

'I'm afraid I am.'

Her face was lifted out of its hiding place as he demanded, 'When?'

She smiled up into his incredulous face. 'Seven months from now.'

'Why have you kept it to yourself all this time?'

Melanie sobered instantly, remembering her unhappiness when she had first discovered she was going to have his child. 'I didn't want you to feel you were under an obligation to continue with our marriage for the baby's sake.'

'My wonderful, crazy darling,' he whispered, tracing the outline of her lips with a gentle, exploratory finger, and she wondered suddenly how she could ever have thought his eyes cold and hard when they looked at her now with such a wealth of love that it made her feel quite faint with happiness. 'We've been such fools, you and I,' he added against her lips. 'Such idiotic fools.'

Time stood still for Melanie in the arms of the man she loved, but a hollow feeling at the pit of her stomach made her draw back a little from him.

'Have you had anything to eat?'

Jason frowned. 'No, I haven't, now that you come to mention it.'

'Are you hungry?'

'Yes. Are you?'

'I'm starving,' she admitted with a mischievous grin. 'Shall we raid the kitchen?'

Laughter lurked in his eyes as he said: 'It sounds like a good idea to me.'

'What are we waiting for, then?' she wanted to know as she slipped off his lap and drew him to his feet, but Jason pulled her back into his arms and kissed her long and satisfyingly before they wandered down the passage towards the kitchen with their arms about each other.

Greystone Manor was ablaze with lights one evening three months later. Jason's generosity had been boundless, and the old house had been transformed into a gracious modern home which Granny Bridget would have been proud of. It was of *her* Melanie was thinking as she came down the stairs that evening, but the sadness in her eyes did not quite diminish the radiance of her appearance.

She found Jason in the living-room mixing their drinks, and at the sight of his tall, imposing figure in a dark evening suit, her face lit up with pleasure.

He turned, sensing her presence, and his warm glance slid down the length of her, taking in the flowing peach-coloured maternity dress that no longer hid her condition.

'Have I told you yet that you're beautiful?' he asked softly, and she laughed shakily, placing a hand against her stomach.

'How can I be beautiful while I look like this?'

'It only makes you look more beautiful to me. Come here.' She went to him without hesitation, and he placed his hands possessively on her hips, drawing her against him. 'Will your lipstick smudge if I kiss you?'

'The sales lady guaranteed that it wouldn't,' she laughed softly, locking her hands behind his head and raising her lips to his.

He kissed her lingeringly, but she stirred against him eventually at the sound of a car coming up the drive.

'Our guests are starting to arrive.'

'A pity,' he murmured against her throat, inhaling the tantalising fragrance of her perfume. 'I'm just beginning to enjoy this.'

'It was *your* idea to have a housewarming party,' she reminded him lightly.

'I must have been out of my mind to suggest it when all I want is to have you to myself.'

'My darling,' she sighed, thrilled by his remark even though she rebuked him gently. 'You're behaving as though we've been married only a few weeks instead of six months.'

Jason raised his head and looked down into her eyes with a hint of the old mockery in his glance. 'Can I help it if you're such a desirable little witch that I want to spend every available moment alone with you?'

The sensuality in his voice sent a familiar weakness through her limbs, but her reply was interrupted by the chiming of the doorbell and, kissing him quickly instead, she disengaged herself from his arms and went through to the hall.

Barnaby Finch stood on the doorstep looking quite unfamiliar in an evening suit. Melanie extended both her hands in welcome, and drew him inside.

'I'm so glad you could come, Barnaby.'

'It was kind of you to invite me, Melanie.' His smile froze as he glanced beyond her. 'Good evening, sir, I'm sorry about that slip.'

'I have no objections to your using my wife's name, Barnaby,' Jason said smoothly, but the arm he placed about Melanie's shoulders was faintly possessive. 'Come through to the living-room and let me mix you a drink.'

The look of relief on Barnaby's face very nearly succeeded in making Melanie laugh out loud, but she smothered the desire hastily when he glanced at her with a curious bewilderment that said clearly, 'I thought for a moment my head would roll.'

The rest of their guests arrived soon afterwards, and Jason, despite his earlier remarks, was a gracious host. At the dinner table that evening, Melanie was seated at the one end, with Mr McAlister and his wife on her right. Barnaby sat on her left with Susan McAlister beside him, and Melanie could not help noticing the interest they seemed to be taking in each other for two people who had met for the first time that evening.

'You know, my dear,' Mr McAlister remarked, capturing Melanie's attention by placing a hand on her arm, 'you're looking lovelier each time I see you, and I don't know what you've done to that husband of yours, but he's certainly mellowed over the past months.' His eyes twinkled mischievously as he added, 'He's mellowed only slightly, mind!'

A warm smile curved Melanie's lips as she glanced down the length of the table to where Jason sat listening intently to something his chief engineer was saying, but he looked up suddenly and, as their eyes met and held, everyone else seemed to fade into insignificance, and they were alone in a private world of their own.

He would, no doubt, always be the arrogant, often ruthless man everyone had come to know, but to her he was the man she loved deeply despite his mockery and cynicism, for underneath it all there lurked a warmth and gentleness intended for her alone. She need never doubt again that his heart belonged to her as wholly as hers belonged to him.

Jason's mouth softened into a brief smile, and hers quivered in response, her heartbeats quickening as his eyes caressed her with a warmth that tinted her cheeks a delicate shade of pink. Then he looked away, and the mask shifted into place as he gave his undivided attention to their guests once more.

They had shared one brief moment together around the crowded table, but they would be alone again later, and Melanie knew she would always find contentment and happiness in that part of him which he reserved only for her.

Harlequin Presents...

The beauty of true romance...

The excitement of world travel...

The splendor of first love...

unique love stories for today's woman

Harlequin Presents...
novels of honest,
twentieth-century love,
with characters who
are interesting, vibrant
and alive.

The elegance of love...
The warmth of romance...
The lure of faraway places...

Six new novels, every
month — wherever
paperbacks are sold.

What readers say about Harlequin Romances

"I feel as if I am in a different world every time I read a Harlequin."
A.T.,* Detroit, Michigan

"Harlequins have been my passport to the world. I have been many places without ever leaving my doorstep."
P.Z., Belvedere, Illinois

"I like Harlequin books because they tell so much about other countries."
N.G., Rouyn, Quebec

"Your books offer a world of knowledge about places and people."
L.J., New Orleans, Louisiana

"Your books turn my...life into something quite exciting."
B.M., Baldwin Park, California

"Harlequins take away the world's troubles and for a while you can live in a world of your own where love reigns supreme."

L.S.. Beltsville. Maryland

"Thank you for bringing romance back to me."

J.W.. Tehachapi. California

"I find Harlequins are the only stories on the market that give me a satisfying romance with sufficient depth without being maudlin."

C.S.. Bangor. Maine

"Harlequins are magic carpets...away from pain and depression...away to other people and other countries one might never know otherwise."

H.R.. Akron. Ohio

*Names available on request

**Make the most of 1980 with your
HARLEQUIN ROMANCE HOROSCOPE and
1980 HARLEQUIN CALENDAR.**

HARLEQUIN READER SERVICE

In U.S.A.
M.P.O. Box 707
Niagara Falls, NY 14302

In Canada
649 Ontario Street
Stratford, Ontario, N5A 6W2

HARLEQUIN SALUTES 1980

Please send me the calendar HARLEQUIN SALUTES 1980. I am
enclosing a check or money order of $3.95 for each calendar ordered,
plus 50¢ to cover postage and handling.

Number of calendars ordered	@ $3.95 each	$_____
N.Y. and N.J. residents add appropriate sales tax		$_____
Postage and handling		$____.50
	TOTAL:	$_____

HARLEQUIN ROMANCE HOROSCOPE

Please send me the following Harlequin Romance Horoscope
volumes. I am enclosing a check or money order of $1.75 for each
volume ordered, plus 40¢ to cover postage and handling.

☐ **Aries**
(Mar. 21-Apr. 20)
☐ **Taurus**
(Apr. 21-May 22)
☐ **Gemini**
(May 23-June 21)
☐ **Cancer**
(June 22-July 22)

☐ **Leo**
(July 23-Aug. 22)
☐ **Virgo**
(Aug. 23-Sept. 22)
☐ **Libra**
(Sept. 23-Oct. 22)
☐ **Scorpio**
(Oct. 23-Nov. 21)

☐ **Sagittarius**
(Nov. 22-Dec. 22)
☐ **Capricorn**
(Dec. 23-Jan. 20)
☐ **Aquarius**
(Jan. 21-Feb. 19)
☐ **Pisces**
(Feb. 20-Mar. 20)

Number of volumes checked @ $1.75 each	$_____
N.Y. and N.J. residents add appropriate sales tax	$_____
Postage and handling	$____.40
TOTAL:	$_____
I am enclosing a grand total of	$_____

NAME_____

ADDRESS_____

STATE/PROV._____ ZIP/POSTAL CODE_____

ROM 2304